Hair
Club
Burning
An Interracial Comedy

Hair Club Burning

An Interracial Comedy

Beth Wareham and Jason Davis

Lisa Hagan Books

ISBN-13: 9780996968621

Library of Congress Control Number: 2015956215

Property: Running Steed Productions
http://www.runningsteedproductions.com

Printed in U.S.A

For the ones who lost their way

And the ones who should have helped.

Contents

PART I 9

PART II...113

PART III..197

AFTERMATH 267

ABOUT THE AUTHORS..273

PART I

Arms pumping and Tory Burch bag swinging wildly,
Mary Ann felt the first drips of sweat hit the water slide
of her butt crack, flowing down to God knows where. It
tickled, a strange sensation when fleeing for one's life.
She was speed walking down the highway double line
in the middle of nowhere, hoping the men behind her
would not shoot.

She couldn't find one person in her life that could
drive out and rescue her. She'd dialed all the friends
and family. No one picked up. She had left the scene
so quickly, so frightened, she hadn't even dialed 911.
Hadn't thought of it, just fled. Later, she'd reflect that all
the sugar she'd eaten had clouded her thoughts, made
her stupid. Deep inside, she knew differently.

She was a woman alone. Wasn't it obvious? What
shit, she thought. I have a family full of men, a phone
full of friends and no one to call at the lowest moment
in recent memory. She pumped her arms faster now,
moving over to the road's shoulder as a car appeared
off in the distance. She figured getting hit by a car instead of a gun blowing a hole in her head was probably
more to her liking. A car could drag you though, her
mind quickly countered. Maybe a gunshot was better.

Periwinkle kitten heels dug into sand and gravel.
Her teeth ground against each other at the sound. She

was creating tiny landslides down the roadside with each step and finally a pump remained behind as she kept moving forward.

Damn, damn, damn she thought as she wheeled around and grabbed the shoe. She was on one leg now, a flamingo with no water, no wings. She knew she looked stupid hopping on one foot in the road in the middle of nowhere. She slipped it back on and strode back to the center of the asphalt, where her shoes worked.

God is punishing me, she thought. For the donuts. I have to die because I ate all those donuts and there is no one to save me. She began muttering words heavenward: "I'll stop the sugar thing," she vowed as her ankle bent outward and she screamed in pain. "I will be more loving." "I'll go to Core Class." She kept walking fast down the centerline and as the car became larger, her thoughts raced. She bit down on her lip again, winced, and a fresh metallic taste of blood filled her mouth.

I'm a bad wife and mother, her inner victim continued. I'm out here because I'm a bad wife and mother. I'm out here because I do things I shouldn't. Her legs were growing tired: She was not at her fittest. I'm out here because I'm selfish. I just had to have what I had to have.

Her thoughts grew even darker and sweat streamed down her body. Mary Ann kept rushing toward the approaching car, her thoughts ripping open her middle-aged soul. She could still hear the men behind her yelling in a language she did not know. She moved even faster, her personal fluids—sweat, tears and snot—attracting molecules of dust from the road. Her face took on the dust's color, a chalky tan her decorator friend would have described as "homosexual putty beige." Why he called it that, she didn't know. The approaching car, she could now see, had a huge hood ornament. Light flashed on it as she moved toward the road's edge again to let it pass.

As the car moved closer, Mary Ann felt a new set of fears well up into the back of her throat. Who would be driving a car like that? She thought. The last time she'd seen one that big and rectangular was in *Goodfellas*. Or was it *American Gangster*? That's it, she thought. The 70s. She realized that the 1970s were coming down a two-lane country highway and were headed directly for her. God, I hated those pantsuits, she thought. And the ties, the pointy collars, the side burns. What is a car like that doing out here in the farmlands of New York? Please God, she bargained again. Let it pass.

The giant yellow Cadillac had another plan. It slowly floated between Mary Ann and the road's shoulder, door swinging open, and a distressed, abandoned middle-aged woman was scooped off burning asphalt and thrown directly into the fire of her life.

◼

Like the hair on her husband's head, Mary Ann's marriage was disappearing. Her life had been fine until the Ring of Fire engulfed her. Her husband's early male patterned baldness had turned these last long months of their marriage into an endless stream of Nizoral, Revita, Nism and Folliguard. With each sad squiggly loss on porcelain, the ring tightened around her life. No hair, no happiness until her husband got what was rightfully his, what God had given him at the beginning of life. Mary Ann's husband wanted his hair back.

Life was okay until one afternoon on the boat when her brother-in-law had said, "Hey Jair! The top of your head looks like a wheat field in winter."

Her husband had whipped around to attack the hurtful comment, taking the wheel of their gleaming white 160 Bowrider Bayliner with him. Three passengers skittered hard right and bounced upward as the boat hit its own wake. Mary Ann could see the rage in her husband's eyes as she fell back hard on her seat.

"Well, what the hell can I do about it?" her husband shot back. "Take Dad and Grandpa to court?"

He was running his hand over his scalp now, back to front, back to front, over and over. This anxious gesture born on this bright day was to become his signature move going forward. Back to front, back to front as he read his computer. Back to front, back to front as he drove. Back to front, back to front as he sat on the couch watching the Jets lose, over and over.

His anger and disappointment over the top of his

head seemed relentless and consuming. Mary Ann needed to help him. After all, she was a girl. Guys ran their hands from back to front. Girls soothed and healed their men. That was the fairy tale she'd been weaned on.

Since that day on the water, Mary Ann had logged onto the Hair Loss Learning Center with him to find help. She researched all aspects, both cultural and scientific, behind the loss of hair in the human male. The Hair Loss Center said, "finding the right hair restoration is like finding the right man or woman for your life."

She repeated this to Jair and he'd asserted "that's right!" They went to work; a heterosexual married couple with a purpose, a project. It wasn't a renovation, but shopping was involved. Special shampoos were ordered and delivered, and for a while seemed useful. Then Jair's scalp turned dry and he cried out over the unfairness of it all. He was bald and now had dandruff! She worried her husband was losing his belief in the world.

She noted every aspect of his hair care on the Hair Loss Log she had downloaded and printed off the Hair Loss Learning Center's website. Propecia was next. All seemed good until his penis couldn't get hard and his breasts became sore. The last symptom she noted in the log was "tender nips." Jair and Mary Ann were getting along, sort-of.

Then he complained and whined and filled the

air with fear and conjecture one time too often. She said, "Maybe you're turning into a girl. I've heard that happens to some white men as they age." She didn't know why she had said it or even what the comment truly meant. She had just said it. Her body felt how ugly a thing it was even as her lips moved, releasing it.

He hadn't spoken to her in three days, so she pulled out the big guns. "Baby, let's just go see a doctor. A real one. One that treats hair and nothing but hair."

He nodded slowly and they went.

◼

Mary Ann could tell immediately that Dr. Sharpe swam in muddy waters. His desk was piled high with papers and his office walls were lined with "before" and "after" pictures that did not resemble each other in the least. A bald Arab head seemed to morph into tidy Caucasian hair with a side part. An Asian woman with a receding hairline next appeared as the same Asian woman, ecstatic beneath a head of flying Roma Gypsy hairs. Dr. Sharpe moved constantly through the piles of files and printouts, fondly casting his glance to the walls where his former patients hung, explaining Jair's hair options.

"But what I recommend to anyone in your condition, Jerald, is the Refined Follicular Unit Grafting which takes care of the hair loss in perpetuity," Dr. Sharpe concluded, turning to look at Mary Ann. "It's my own procedure and it will keep your husband evergreen, as they say."

Why this last had been directed at her, Mary Ann didn't know. But Dr. Sharpe's head swung the other way so quickly, she wasn't truly sure he had been looking at her. And who were "they" that "say" husbands with hair were evergreen? Woman kept bald men around all the time, she mused.

"This procedure is not inexpensive and not without risk," Dr. Sharpe was now bearing down on Jair. "But I can promise you that I'll put thousands of hairs back on Jerald's head."

Her husband's face lit up.

"Thousands of hairs," the Doctor repeated, as he turned to face Mary Ann.

"Thousands!" Jair blubbered.

This guy, Mary Ann thought. What a used car salesman. He had just offered her desperate husband hairs without telling her how much they cost. Outrageous! Jair had gotten those shiny eyes and his mouth got all wet when Dr. Sharpe had said 'thousands of hairs.'

It was look she once knew well, that shiny-eyed, wet-slack-mouth face. He had looked that way in bed the night they had married. Hell, for years, he looked that way every time she was nude, semi-nude, or completely not nude.

What she said was "Will you guarantee it will work? Will Jair have hair? Will you promise that Jerald will have a full head of hair for the rest of his life?"

"Well, no," Dr. Sharpe answered from behind the chaotic surfaces of his desk. "I cannot promise that; promising that is against the laws of the State of New York. I cannot say I can cure cancer either. But what I know is my experience, and my experience tells me that your husband's future includes hair. Hair that I can give him. Hair that will resemble his because it IS his. It will last forever and look great, even soaked with pool water."

"Pool water!" her husband exclaimed, shiny eyes locked on the Doctor.

She didn't feel the same sense of excitement. "Why won't the water pull his hairs out?"

"Because I graft his hair from a populated scalp area to an unpopulated scalp area," Dr. Sharpe explained in a "voilà!" kind of way. "I fuse his hairs from a heavily forested region of scalp in the back onto the smooth planes of his upper forehead, the area we call the "balding launch zone". I take his hairs, bisect them once, twice, keeping the follicle completely intact. Then I insert the hairs from his back scalp into his front scalp, thus populating his entire head. I have perfected the surgical technique over many decades. It is part Science, part Art. I will return to you the vibrant man you married." His smile was huge and flat and fake and aimed right at Jair.

He followed the Doctor's every move.

"What is the cost?" she said, feeling like the skunk

at the picnic. Then, a darker image grabbed her: 'Here, in this tiny room with these two men, I am the Third Wheel. What if they start kissing? What do I do?' She shook her head to toss off the thought. Why had she begun to feminize her husband so often in her thoughts? It couldn't be a sign the marriage was growing stronger.

"It depends," said the doctor, diving deep into his cloudy, paper-strewn world. "I'll have to run tests. Make projections. I can approximate the number of hairs I'll need, but not how many hairs Jerald's head will actually accept."

"I accept them all!" Jair cried, smiling like a baby with gas.

"His head has to accept the hairs?" she asked. "How do you know it will? Why not use a donor head? You get hairs that are compatible with Jair's without taking his good hairs. Does Jair's scalp attach to the new hairs immediately?"

"Every patient is unique," Doctor Sharpe said as he stood and walked back over to the window. "He will not have a donor: We work with his remaining hairs. We harvest hair from the back of his head where the hairs are abundant. We reinsert some to the Balding Launch Zone. This is intense handwork done under a microscope and requires an artisan's skill. These reinserted hairs will take time to root into Jerald's scalp, just like a flower taking root in nutritious soil," he said turning back to her.

He stared deeply into the window and both he and his reflection said, "Every patient leaves here with hair." The effect was powerful and the word "hair" seemed to hang in the air just above their heads.

"So how much does it cost again?" she asked. "As I said, hard to say. My best estimate is that he is going to need at least 1500 hairs. As I work, I will make adjustments. I must find the trace lines of your husband's past hair and restore the follicles so that all works in concert. It's not easy nor is it quick. But he will be restored."

"So," she said as she leaned forward in her chair and felt her heart beat, "is 1500 hairs a lot of hairs?"

"Some patients need only hundred of hairs, others 1500. Some need 3000, 4000 hairs but that is extreme," Dr. Sharpe replied.

"That's a lot, isn't it?" Mary Ann agreed. "How much will Jerald's 1500 hairs cost, Doctor?"

Dr. Sharpe let out a long stream of air that whistled down and out his nostrils. "It's ten dollars a hair," he said in a perfect American accent. He stared out the window for several heartbeats longer and turned toward her.

"Ten dollars a hair!" she exclaimed. She had no idea how much money 1500 hairs times $10 added up to be, but already she knew it was a lot.

She could hear Jair shifting in his seat before he bellowed, "I don't care how much it costs! I want my hair back! I work hard! I want hair! Nobody cares how

I feel about how I look! I just go to work! Work! Work! Work! With no hair!" He was winded and losing outrage as he searched for oxygen. The outburst was over. "But I care" he said as he sat. "I care a lot."

"Of course I want you to look your best, honey," Mary Ann said, feeling shamed for appearing to deny her husband the happiness of hair. "But that's a great deal of money for something that we don't even know will work. Remember the Propecia?"

"Forget that!" Jair exclaimed with a force that caused his wife's eyes to blink shut hard and fly open. "A hair grafted to my head is not going to cause breast tenderness. He paused and she saw him flush slightly. "Let's do this thing!"

He was on his feet now, hands jammed deep into his khaki cargo shorts, already fingering car keys and two disks that felt like rogue Mentos. Jair's mood had changed so violently, she had felt the air pressure shift in the wee messy office.

Mary Ann looked back at the Doctor. "This procedure will cost $10 times 1500 hairs. Is that correct? That's it, isn't it? 10 x 1500? That's a lot. Yup, that's a lot of money, Doctor." She swiveled to face her husband, "That's a lot of money, dear. That's a year of college for our son."

"Oh, I know," Jair cut in. His eyes had lost their shine and his lips were dry. Everyday Jair was back in the room. "But I've got to do this. I feel it. I have to do this and I promise I will make up the $15,000 with a couple of extra quick deals. I'll get us back to even in no time. But this is the rest of my life we are talking about here."

With that, her husband reclaimed the examination room and said yes to the procedure.

Next Tuesday it was 8:00 a.m. sharp for hair assessment, then surgery at 9:00.

◘

Mary Ann came to think of this period in her life as The Restoration Drama. Though Jair wore no brocade or long powdered wigs, his obsession with regaining his unremarkable-to-begin-with hair covered everything they owned and did. Hairs and thoughts of hairs popped up everywhere. A squiggle on the kitchen counter turned out to be one of his lost hairs and her sweater picked his hairs off the couch. She found one of his business cards in between the front seats of his SUV. He had scrawled the word "hair" over his own name. Short dark man hairs infiltrated her handbag. She felt dirty but not good dirty, like naked-man-dirty. Dirty, like we-need-Clorox- and a-long-handled-tool dirty.

Jair's hair, Mary Ann thought, was the least of his troubles. They'd begun screwing in college like two of those monkeys with the red butts that she saw on the Nat Geo channel. Now, here they were, sitting in a doctor's office being robbed because of hair.

Overall, Mary Ann liked Jair just fine and was

usually glad she married him. He made money and was rarely drunk. Sure he was bald, but he could be sexy.

She'd seen it and knew it to be true. Thoughts of 1998 still made her flush with remembered heat.

But what she really felt for Jair now was a deep maternal love. Freud had been right: You have to feel the mommy love to stay. Alas, mommy love ran off the hot red monkey butt feelings, sometimes completely. They were now just two unremarkable people sitting on a couch discussing what they should watch, a New England Cape being renovated or the Hitler Channel.

Where are those monkeys, she thought as she watched her husband leave the room. I would give up all that I have and all that I am for one more glimpse of that fabulous engorged red butt.

◼

They were watching television two nights later and he blurted, "My brother and I are sooo different," then looked back at the game and smirked.

"How so," she'd asked, hating herself for playing along.

"His bald spot started on the back of his head and mine started in the front." Jair's hands were cupped hovering over different parts of his skull, fingers spread, as he demonstrated these wildly divergent phenomena—balding from the front backwards and balding from the back forwards. She heard Jair tell the story, once again, of how he and his brother went bald.

As they moved through the weekend toward Tuesday morning, Jair became highly excited. He seemed to be everywhere at once in the house and always in her way. She caught him twice, in what they called 'The Duck Room," rearranging his antique decoy ducks. He and his father had started the collection. Why, she didn't know. Jair's father couldn't get out of a club chair by himself, no less hunt for waterfowl. It's where Jair watched television now, surrounded by unmoving bright green- headed ducks.

Once a year, Mary Ann bought him a very expensive wooden bird so he could enlarge his collection. She resented it. She'd even bought him a huge Canadian goose whittled by an unknown folk artist between 1950 and 1959. This mid-century modern decoy had set her back four figures. She'd gasped when she opened the credit card bill. It was easy to forget those silly looking old toys could go for hundreds of thousands of dollars. But they did keep him occupied. Should be grateful for that, she thought. By Sunday night, she worried he'd boil over.

"....Mom knew this day was coming! She predicted it!" he said as he moved through the room, bringing his phone up to his ear as he walked. He kept on going through the back door and she saw him next on the back terrace, yapping away and gesturing upward with one long index finger. Thank goodness that glass is protecting me, she thought. That man is insane.

Mary Ann didn't know who Jair was talking to, didn't care. She figured it was Peter, his butt-of-a-woman brother who was the biggest pussy she had ever met. I married bald brothers, she thought as she stood up off the couch. I married bald whiny brothers and the joke's on me. Why hadn't I just married a guy with allergies?

She walked out of the living room and down the hall toward her room. Her son's door was shut and she could hear his laugh. The boy was IM'ing, texting, or beating off. Same difference, she thought. As she walked into her room, HER ROOM as she had insisted to Jair, she wondered if all marriages felt like child rearing. She had no idea. She had only married this one guy and didn't have enough data.

Mary Ann was tall, five foot eleven, and had what her husband called "the body of a race horse, only… nice tits." She ate a lot and only recently had gained a little weight. But just a little. Her legs still stopped traffic. She did have three deep lines on her neck. She had turned forty and young men started stopping her on the street. One went so far as to ask her to be his "cougar" and she had felt both flattered and offended. On any given day, she believed her now 44-year body was hotter than any Conde Nast intern could ever achieve. All in all, she was right.

Her doctor had told her she was in peri-meno-pause. In the years leading up to menopause, Mary

Ann would feel no other symptom to her body's shifting hormonal landscape except for a heightened, almost rabid desire to mount men half her age. She didn't even see her male contemporaries any more. Too old, she thought, slow penile recovery time.

A baldhead made her skin crawl—a sensation just like a hot flash except it took a lot longer to go away. A fat, Astrodome-type stomach on a man signaled he'd completely given up. Much more so than wearing Crocs or New Balance, she'd decided. She really hated giving up. Most of this hungry searching, observing and philosophizing went on in the streets or subways of New York, two of the greatest pick-up spots in the history of human kind.

She sat at the glistening counter of her en suite bathroom and began wiping off makeup with tiny pads of cotton. She still liked her face, even the neck. Sure, there were lines here and there. Her jawline was worrisome, especially where it turned in toward the chin. She watched that bend for the tiny pads of jowl, a condition she associated with Early American portraiture and her mother's friends. Not here, she vowed, as if fighting off an ISIS insurgency or nesting bees.

Who are these middle-aged women who feel invisible, she'd think as she flirted her way across town. She had never seen so many young available men. She'd look and look and look, but at the end of each day, she'd go home to bald. Why don't you just do it, she'd think every day. Why don't you just grab one of these guys.

But, she'd always leave the city without doing much of anything. She'd told everybody standing there that day—the day of the long white dress with a train - that she would honor Jair. In the end, that's exactly what she was going to do.

She bore down on her face with another tiny cotton pad, pulling out a daub of black goo from the inner eye. Painted lady with your painted face, she thought. Who warned the world about make-up, she wondered. The Bible? Shakespeare? The pile of cotton rounds, some red, some blue, some black were piling up in front of her.

As sexy as she felt, Mary Ann understood on a deep level that she was not Marilyn Monroe. She considered herself a pragmatist, a woman of science. She dealt in realities, was a Wife and a Mother. Mary Ann knew there had to be a reason for the young male verbal discharges of lust. She didn't just start glowing one day in a size 12 and every dude under the age of 25 noticed.

She suspected she was secreting estrogen at an alarming rate (for God's sake, her shins had started sweating) and inexperienced animals simply caught her scent in the air. She thought a female hormonal signal was a female hormonal signal, no matter what age it oozed out of. On a molecular level, she smelled like a newly menstruating 14 year-old.

Stay married, she'd tell herself. Stay married because it has never been and will never be about a man's hair. Stay married, she thought. We're a good team. Even in a shit storm of estrogen, Mary Ann was going to honor her commitments, even the ones made so many years ago.

Stay married. We have a son to educate. You've gotten this far, don't screw up the kid. Stay married.

Sex just isn't that important. Men, especially the young ones, would make your life hell or bore you to death. Stay married. Because if you start this sex thing up again, who knows where it will end? Stay married. Grow up.

Do what you said you would do. He could be so much worse, even with hair.

Mary Ann set down the cotton streaked with the beige of her foundation. She looked down at the brightly colored pile of dirty wipes and back up at her face in the mirror. She smiled and her eyes grew bright.

◼

At first light on Tuesday, Mary Ann heard her husband singing in the bathroom. *Sweet Child O' Mine.* Horrible. The big day was here—Jair was getting hair!—and he would require a long toilette this morning.

Mary Ann rolled over and scissored her legs the entire width of the bed. The long married never had enough bed, she thought. Her left hip popped and it felt good, a relief from pressure she didn't even know she felt. Get him through this, she thought. Then I'll work on me.

The bathroom door swung open so hard it hit the bedroom wall.

"Oh....oh...SORRY!" Jair boomed, filling the room with heat and moisture.

"I'm awake," she said, staring at the far wall. "Oh, great. I didn't want to wake you but I couldn't sleep. It's been going on a long time now and I didn't want to burden you with this problem on top of the hair problem."

Jeez, she thought. It never stops, this list of husband ills. She knew he was eating, farting and pooping. Any woman who married a man could expect to do battle with these dark forces, day in and day out.

"It was like I was telling you last night," he smiled over at her. "I really haven't been sleeping well. I get in the bed and BOOM! Wide awake."

"Maybe you don't sleep because you're worried about your hair...or the hair that you don't have— that's maybe a better way to say it."

"Funny!" he said. A comment that would usually have sent him sniveling into a hankie had just flown over him, not leaving any kind of a dent. "Nothing can get me down today," he said as he went back into the mists of the master bath.

Mary Ann pulled her legs together and rolled off the bed into a standing position. She stood in her t-shirt, the "I <heart> Hitachi Wands" one that her girlfriend had given her and wondered why she'd gotten a t-shirt rather than the thing itself.

"Faux-shizzle!" he yelled from beyond the wall of hot wet air.

The thing itself, the thing itself, she thought as she crossed the room. Her husband wanted hair but she wanted him to not be boring. She wanted him to think and talk of other things, not just hair, ducks and the Jets.

She wanted him to look at her like he looked at Dr. Sharpe, like he looked when they were young, all wet lipped and interested. She wanted attention. Direct, hot attention followed by a cool comfortable silence in which to bathe. She wanted to feel like marriage was more than a commitment to send a kid to college or resurface a driveway.

"You drive!" he chirped. "I'm the patient!"

Good grief, she thought. He thinks he's having a heart transplant! She walked over to the dresser and pulled out jeans and a tank top.

"I believe we only have to worry about that on the drive back," she said.

After all the work of growing, she never understood why Jair so loved being treated like a child. It never failed though. He loved being coddled, driven, fed, lulled, rocked, petted, stroked and entertained. She had even found his friends for him. Was he lazy or did he just think this was the work of women? She didn't know and had stopped trying to figure it out. It was simply too exhausting. Especially on a Tuesday, just past dawn, when your husband was getting ready to receive hair.

◼

Dr. Sharpe's waiting room was filled to capacity at 8:00 a.m. The ride had been uneventful except for when Jair had gotten ahold of the automatic lock button on the driver's side, flicking it up and yelling "Safe!" before flicking it down and croaking "Sorry!" over and over again.

"Good morning," the receptionist said. "Here for some hair?" she smiled at Jair. He smiled back.

She swiveled in her chair, took a clipboard off the pile, and swiveled back, still smiling at him. "I'll need your insurance card as well."

Mary Ann cut through the twisted eyebeams and said, "Can I please have that?" and took the clipboard out of the woman's hand. She crossed the room and sat in the far corner where two chairs were free.

Jair remained at the counter talking to the receptionist. Mary Ann noticed his lips were wet again. She knew they were talking about hair. She was relieved she didn't have to listen.

The final line of the form said "payment" and she jammed her hand into her handbag. Phone. Checkbook. Pencil. Tic Tics. She knew the feel of it all from endless purse safaris. Her fingers tightened on the wallet and soon she had a MasterCard in hand.

Despite her constant yearning to couple with men half her age, Mary Ann was a bit of a Pollyanna. She knew the card was clean because she had just paid it down to around $500. Visa had increased her credit limit and she knew it was something like $20,000. She was scrupulous about paying bills and insisted she always have her own credit.

She remembered the follicle math. 1500 hairs times 10 dollars = $15,000 with a little wiggle room should Jair require more hairs. She began to write in the name on the card, card number, expiration date and sneaky code off the back. She signed the bottom of the form; she was now responsible for all incurred hair fees for Jair's hair from this moment forward. In addition, should Jair succumb to wounds received during the hair transplant, that seemed to be on her too. She felt the responsibility and it enraged her.

She had never put this much money on her credit card ever. They had slowed their use of plastic after the 2007/08 crash. It was fine with her: She'd not understood a word since they moved all the customer service reps to Mumbai anyway. Mumble on High, India, she called it. Jair talked to her about interest rates and hidden fees.

They agreed: Pay cash. This became a teaching moment for their son—the old delayed gratification lecture/ demonstration—and she felt no compulsion to use the card. Ever. Not even when Tory Burch flats were 30% off and matched her bag perfectly.

Until now. No choice. Back against the wall. If Jair didn't close his wet mouth about his hair, she was going off the Tappan Zee Bridge. Or worse. A flash of herself dangling at the end of one of Jair's Christmas ties flickered behind her eyes and passed. Or maybe, she'd go to his man cave and sit there until his man fumes overwhelmed her. She would stumble out, gasping for air, and die on the kitchen floor, next to the dishwasher. This hit—putting $15,000 on a credit card—she was taking for her family and she prayed he'd honor the marital ledger and pay her back.

Air moved and metal scrapped metal as Jair sat in his chair next to Mary Ann.

"She was so nice!" Jair said as his eyes glistened in his wife's direction. "She says there will be no pain. And see that guy over there? He's scheduled to get 3200 hairs grafted today! That's a lot, isn't it Honey?"

"Oh, that's a big one alright," she said in a flat voice. "But what's the difference? Oh, I know, about ten grand, right? Take this form to your new girlfriend. I'm going to sit here and sleep."

◼

Jair returned to his seat. He was fidgeting and started the HA-HANK! throat clearing that signaled excitement, anger or hurt. He hadn't done it for a while, since the last Jets game probably. He was too concerned with pulling his hands across his baldhead, back to front, back to front. Now, he was doing the HA-HANK! and back-to- front, back-to-front. She figured his stress was huge.

Well join the club, Buddy, she thought. As you wiggle like a toddler over your shiny head, I drive you around and listen to you go HA-HANK! as twenty sad bald sacks in a waiting room turn to see who made the HA-HANK! sound. I give you this day of my life and all you can say is HA-HANK!

"Jerald Carlyle? Jerald Carlyle?" the receptionist shouted into the room.

Jair rose quickly, let out a HA-HANK! as he tugged at the waist of his shorts, bent, kissed her quickly on the cheek, and crossed the room.

As he passed in front of the counter, Mary Ann saw the bright flash of his teeth as he arrived at the receptionist. She saw the door to the doctor's offices swing open and shut, suddenly hiding whoever was making that annoying throat-clearing noise. She looked down at her lap and listened to Ha-HANK! as it grew softer, then silent. Jair was down the hall now, almost to the room where he would be reunited with his long lost head of hair. She was praying it would work and this hell would be over. She was praying for their life to return to normal. She wanted to focus on what they did have.

Mary Ann caught herself praying for hair.

■

"Where's Doctor Sharpe?" Jair asked the receptionist as he was led back into the cluster of offices, waiting areas and procedure rooms.

"He's here," she said. "But because he can't work on everyone, your restoration will be done by Doctor Bahdoon Bahdoon Samatar. He's one of our best."

They were halfway down a long hallway, passing at least ten rooms filled with animated bald patients meeting their saviors.

"Doctor Baboon Baboon?" Jair said, knowing he wasn't even close.

The receptionist smiled. "He gets that a lot," she said. She slowed and stopped and said, "Doctor Bahdoon Bahdoon Samatar, can get sensitive about his name. He's from Somalia."

"Somalia?" Jair was amazed.

"Yes, Somalia," she said. "Let's practice: Bah-doon Bah-doon Sam-A-tar."

"Isn't that where the pirates are? The country that ate the helicopters?"

"Ate the helicopters?" the receptionist repeated. "What are you talking about, sir?"

"Never mind," Jair said. "If he's got my hair, he's my guy!"

She smiled, turned and pushed a door open. Jair followed her in. On one side of the room, a nurse with short brown hair was bent over, looking into a cupboard. On the other side, all Jair could see was the back of a lab coat.

"Oh, hellooooo," came over the sound of running water. "I be with da gentleman one moment."

"You'll love them," the receptionist smiled. "Everyone does. Muriel and Dr. Bahdoon Bahdoon Samatar have nothing but happy customers!" Before Jair answered, she was gone.

Turning from the sink, Dr. Bahdoon Bahdoon Samatar looked at Jair with a blinding smile. His skin was deep black, his thin body and face all angles. His teeth looked huge, fake and powered by electricity.

Above the smile, his head did not have one hair. "Dr. Barton," Jair said, extending his hand. "Dr. Bahdoon Bahdoon Samatar" the Doctor corrected as he shook Jair's hand. "Where I come from, our names honor our father and grandfather."

"Dr. Bardon, then. Nice to meet you!" Jair said. The smell of rubbing alcohol began to bite into his nostrils.

"Dr. Bahdoon Bahdoon Samatar. In my country, we use three names. Is pleasing to meet you, Jerald."

"You too, Doc! How about I just call you 'Doc'?"

"Dr. Bahdoon Bahdoon Samatar is my name and in my country, we use three names." The good hair doctor said, smiling so brightly Jair felt pain. "Shall we begin to your hair?"

"'To my hair?' Well yes. I've been looking forward to this!" Jair sat in the seat he knew to be the patient's.

He felt the thin dark man move in behind his head. Nurse Muriel stepped in front of his chair and stared.

"Ha yes. Patients love hair," Dr. Bahdoon Bahdoon Samatar replied.

"Why don't you have hair?" Jair said over his shoulder? "Of all people, I thought you'd have a lot!"

"I shave skull," the Doctor said. "In my country, hair is not big problem. No, you will feel stick," the blackest person Jair had ever seen said. "You will feel stick then head goes no."

"Head goes no?" Jair said into the air above his head. He could no longer see his bald black doctor behind him.

"Your head will not feel the insertions made by Dr. Bahdoon Bahdoon Samatar after he puts a local anesthetic into your scalp. That's what he means by 'no'. He means you won't feel anything," Muriel said.

With this, Dr. Bahdoon Bahdoon Samatar struck. His long hypodermic slid under skin once hidden from the world by hair. Jair's forehead wrinkled as a specific burning, a laser-pointed pain, burrowed into the top of his head. He let out a "whoosh" of air.

"Worst part!" the Doctor said. Muriel quickly agreed.

"Hurts," Jair said.

"Yes, hurt," the Doctor repeated.

Muriel didn't say a word. She thought all these hair-chasers were soft. The needle always freaked them out. Wait until you see what's next, she thought. Then she smiled to herself as she crossed the room to sit down and wait.

◘

Jair sat in the chair waiting for his scalp to go numb. An urge to put his hand on the back of his head and pull it forward, back to front, back to front, overtook him and he got a few strokes in before Dr. Bahdoon Bahdoon Samatar's voice cut in.

"You feel my touch on your head. Some light. Some not. All is good. I drew hairs then I will make incision and hair goes in. Will be good."

He leaned over Jair's head with a Sharpie black pen and went to work. He drew lines radiating from Jair's deforested region all the way back to the last stand of thin hairs. He gently bent Jair's hairs with his long fluttery fingers that tapered to a soft point. The Doctor was assessing Jair's hair growth direction.

After fifteen minutes of fluttering and drawing and walking around Jair and sighing, Dr. Bahdoon Bahdoon Samatar's thumb and forefinger made a circle and he flicked his finger hard on Jair's scalp.

"Ouch!" Jair shouted at Muriel across the room. "Ah, you still feel!" the Doctor smiled at Jair. "Few minutes more and nothing. Then we cut!"

Muriel got busy taking scalpels, needles and thin, delicate-looking hooks with sharp points out of drawers. She laid them on the steel table by Jair. It looked like the contents of a cobbler's kit, circa 1848.

She knew this guy in the khaki shorts wasn't worldly enough to be afraid of a Somali with a knife. Somalis were a fierce people and she took endless delight watching the tiny Sunni doctor work over gigantic American men.

A big American man had left Muriel two years ago and she still couldn't get his smell out of her studio apartment on Lex and 97th. It was an ongoing process, she told herself, this purging and healing. She knew the day she no longer smelled her ex-husband would be the day she was free.

Muriel faced Jair. His wet lips parted and he said, "will this hurt?" She just smiled as if to say, "it'll hurt a wuss like you...."

She waited a beat and then, "No, it won't hurt," fell out of her mouth and onto Jair. He smiled.

The Doctor was preparing himself for the show.

He put on a surgical mask and over it, the kind of facemask a welder might wear. A long flat piece of plastic protected his nose and mouth and two rectangles sat over each eye, lenses magnifying his huge black eyes until they seemed to take up half his face. Jair thought Dr. Bahdoon Bahdoon Samatar looked like a beetle he'd seen under a microscope in high school.

"We begin!" the doctor said too loudly. Jair blinked, Muriel smiled and the doctor leaned over Jerald, scalpel and a long, hooked needle in hand.

The Doctor put the scalpel at the top of Jair's

forehead and pulled it from front to back in a slow sure movement, a quarter inch deep. It was poetry really, Muriel thought.

"Gash-damn-mother-gah-STOP!" Jair exploded from his chair. His eyes were almost as large as the Doctor's and his face was bright red.

"That HURTS ME!" Jair said, eyes glistening to the point of tears. "That hurts me," he repeated softly as he looked to the floor and licked his already wet lips.

"Sorry. Sorry," the Doctor said. "Muureal, more anesthetic please! Our patient is too strong for us and needs more!" he laughed.

Jair swore that this time he felt the needle hit and bounce off his skull. The sting was followed by a warm feeling spreading across his head and face.

Muriel walked around Jair and handed him a tiny white cup of paper and said, "This will further relax you and numb any pain in your skull."

Jair threw the contents of the cup back like tequila and then said, "let's bo dis ting."

Muriel turned away and thought, Sure thing, GI Joe. What she said was, "He's almost ready, Doctor. His speech is eroding."

Ten minutes passed and the Doctor again flicked Jair's skull with his forefinger. No response.

Bahdoon Bahdoon Samatar made his move.

◘

Dr. Bahdoon Bahdoon Samatar picked the scalpel up and sliced into the top of Jair's forehead. Then, in another smooth, completely confident stroke, the Doctor turned the scalpel back from the head's crown and radiated an incision from back to front. Then another incision, again back to front. This continued until Jair had long precise cuts that looked like sunbeams pulsating across the top of his head.

Muriel leaned over Jair as the doctor worked and began dabbing beads of blood off his skull. His eyes were large and bright and his moist lips were moving. He was either praying or singing and Muriel suspected it was the latter. Sure, he wore the big khaki shorts just like her ex but Muriel didn't take him for one of those lumbering Bible-types. You rarely found those this close to New York City.

"....you pull me close....I just say no...." Jair sang into the middle of the small airless room.

"What he say?" the Doctor laughed as he drew the scalpel from back to front. "He's funny!"

"...oh but when we kiss...oh....FIRE!....." Jair continued.

"He's as high as my ex-husband" Muriel said and the Doctor smiled again. "Hopefully not as stupid."

"Oh, he doesn't know things," the Doctor said as he threaded the first one quarter of one of Jair's hairs onto the long needle with the hooked end. "At least not at the moment!" the Doctor laughed as he swooped in and tucked the hook inside Jair's incision. "Now, you stay leetle hair!" Bahdoon Bahdoon Samatar smiled as he reached toward the tiny container of soon-to-be-implanted follicles.

"….But when we kiss, kisses like Sampson and Delilah….Oh when we kiss…FIRE…." Jair sang.

For the rest of the morning, Jair's weak voice bleated out mangled Bruce Springsteen lyrics as Doctor and Nurse worked together. Bent over, the two seemed to read each other's thoughts, completing hair insertions wordlessly and perfectly until Jair had tiny black cuts covering the front of his head.

When he was finally given a hand mirror, Jair was still high. He looked at himself and shouted, "Noooooooooooo! Noooooo! I have no hair! Where's the hair!! NOO! I want my wife! Where's mah hair? Hair Nurse!"

"Mr. Jerald, MR. JERALD!" Doctor Bahdoon Bahdoon Samatar shouted. "The hair grow! This isn't wig! This must grow!"

Jair looked back at his scalp, now a huge expanse of skin covered with beads of blood, exposed follicles and nubs.

"I want hair!" His eyes filled: He dreamed of awaking, a kind of male Cinderella with Rapunzel's hair. Jair was another victim of fairy tales.

"Mr. Carlyle!" Muriel said sternly. "Surely you understand that hair must be grown. You'll have a head of hair in 6 to 8 months. But this isn't a tricycle under the Christmas tree! Hair restoration is no given! You must work for it. Keep your hair well and it will grow. Mistreat it and it will leave."

Just like me, Muriel the Hair Nurse thought. "I'll leave you two now and meet you later, Mr. Carlyle, in office," the Doctor said as he left the room."

"Okay, Jerald," Muriel sighed." Let's get you up and out of here and back to your wife."

■

She was being pulled up through green murk and dirt. Bits of roots and algae swirled around her. She saw a circle of gorgeous firemen above her, pulling her hair hand over hand ever so slowly. She realized through the strange sensations that she was trapped. She was in a hole in the ice or maybe a well. Young male faces with unblinking black eyes stared down at her through the water as she raised her arms toward the light. None of them spoke. With each gentle pull, the firemen's lips moved, a murmur of horror as her hair grew a foot or two, dropping her deeper into the hole.

She felt herself slide over the black and green rocks as she sunk deeper. Her hands tried to grab ahold of something. Failing, she reached toward the young men working so hard to save her.

"PULL!" Mary Ann shouted into the pillow she clutched as the glaring white light of the sun hit her bedroom wall at 6:30 a.m. on Wednesday morning.

She sunk back down into the pillows. What is real?

she thought, looking around the room. She heard the shower in the master bath. Okay, Jair was up and going to work. Excellent. She heard the shower tap shut off, a thump and then nothing. Further away, a buzzer fired rhythmically. Her son would be up soon. He was really real, she thought as she closed her eyes again. I need to give him some attention. Yes, I do. But Jair's hair. She rolled to the right and kept going until the soles of her feet hit rug.

"Grrrr-ate!" Her husband said as he appeared in the bedroom, again shrouded in the hot shower mists of time. Every morning, just like this, he would appear in the center of the bedroom all moist and energetic.

Every morning. Forget that movie, she thought. Life IS ground hog day. That's what's real. The sameness.

"I feel GRRRRRR-ate!" Jair said as he did that little dance with the towel rubbing across his back. "I feel great and soon I'll look great, thanks to you!"

He gave her a quick kiss as he passed by the bed on his way to the closet. He radiated heat and the smell of coconut. She noticed the tiny black specks all over his head where the incisions were made. Pink tendrils of abused scalp crisscrossed the Hair Launch Zone. A pimple crested white on the side of his nose. He'll put on the Donna Karan suit, she guessed, so he looks extra nice for work.

"So glad," she said as she walked toward her own closet. "So glad you feel good today."

"I feel so good I'll drive the boy," Jair said. "I feel so

good I'll drive the boy and you can just stay here and do what you want to do."

"That's so..."

"My pleasure!" he yelled as Donna Karan side vents flapped in time with his strides out the door, son in tow, towards his Lexus SUV.

◾

By late morning, she had done the thing she vowed not to do again. This time, the repercussions weren't felt just on her waistline but through every vein of her life.

Around 10:30 a.m. that morning, Mary Ann was at the end of the driveway when she turned the wheel of the car hard right without thinking. Left was always quicker to town, but this way meant something else. The Sugar Express was running, her one fail-safe, feel-good activity that didn't involve alcohol or credit cards and always meant fun. No one ever saw her; she drove the back roads.

For much of her marriage, when she'd hit a certain level of internal frustration and distress, she would take to the road, driving and eating. She'd head for the country beyond all the houses with a passenger seat full of pleasure: Mike and Ikes, Dunkin, M&Ms, Krispys, tubs of blue slurpees, fireballs, Hob Nails and Spree.

Sometimes she'd get ethnic, filling the seat with

coconut covered chocolates and lemon jellied slices. She thought of this as her trip to the Caribbean.

Other times she'd load up on butter pastry, imaging her car was a barge and the New York farmland the outskirts of Prague. She'd stopped this secret life when she realized she had graduated from size ten to twelve. The added mound of fat between her belly button and pudendum alarmed her. So she stopped.

Today is different, she thought. Today is different and I deserve this because Jair and his hair have driven me mad. I've heard nothing else for months. Today is different because I have not done this in over a year.

Today is different. I need to do this today. Her blood stream awash in sugar, the speed and light of a fast drive would send her to another world, a world where she looked great in low-rise jeans and could play guitar.

She drove past block after block of suburban houses that retailed for three-quarters of a million for a dump to $5 million, if the wind was blowing in the right direction. Yards were landscaped with a precision that bordered on violence. Hedges were all perfect angles and spheres. Flowerbeds did not spill their borders.

Ornamental trees abounded. She often fantasized about leaving a flat bed truck full of watermelons or mangoes or an abandoned refrigerator on one of these front lawns.

She thought about grabbing the more annoying

yard decor: the Palmer's huge metal wind chimes or those horrible bright white twin arbors the Glassman's jammed in between driveway and house. She fought off an impulse to toss the red gazing ball through the Arundi's plate glass window.

At Empire Street, she made another right and there she was at the end-of-the-world for the middle- aged woman: An adobe-looking strip mall. In it were the seeds of the modern 44-year-old American woman's undoing: The ever-stretching waistbands of Chico's. Cookie bouquets. The Multiplex. The spry look of Aerosols. Zale's' Eternity Bands. The untenable vanilla smell of inexpensive body lotion. Card shops. Sees Candies. Scented candles.

She slid into the parking lot and without hesitation; she got out of her car and crossed the wide cement walk. She strode head on into the most dangerous commercial venue in this axis of evil. Funny, she thought. It didn't feel like handling a viper, walking the plank or having a last cigarette while tied to a pole. It felt like stepping into the sun.

The smell hit her and she felt the familiar rush. This smell, the sheer strength and complexity of it entranced her as no waft of Cinnabon ever could. This smell put the gooey insides of even a giant chocolate chip cookie to shame. This smell moved her. This smell was the smell of deep-fried cake.

She didn't know what she loved more, the pretty pinks or whites or reds glistening on the rack, or the smell of manipulated, boiled and baked sugar. Sugar worked deeply on the human organism, she noticed.

Sugar somehow got on one's skin and sunk down in. Once bitten, it haunted and called. A person could feel it spread through the veins, leaving a glow on all it touched. Mary Ann loved sugar, fought the craving constantly, and knew that an Almond Joy, 2 bags of Peanut M&Ms and some Fireballs could cure a broken heart. Sure you crashed later, but what a ride.

Everything was so orderly. Circles were spaced equidistant from one another, oozing shiny frosting down their sides. Small tan and white balls were left in heaps on the lowest shelf. Steel surfaces gleamed everywhere.

Dunkin Donuts was Mary Ann's happy place.

For years, she'd tuck a box or two under her arms when she went to fundraising meetings and volunteer mixers. She'd eat one donut with some fanfare and, during the course of the meeting manage to eat a second and third while business was conducted. As the group broke apart, she'd often take a fourth donut and remark, "Oh, we got so much work done I might as well reward myself and have two!"

Today was different. She hadn't breathed in months and today, this day, this not-Groundhog-Day day was hers to do differently. She was no longer walking the razor's edge of Jair's hair. She was, this day, free.

She stepped to the counter and said, "I'd like 2 Chocolate Frosted, 2 of the Chocolate Glazed, 2 plain glazed, 2 Bavarian Creams and 2 jelly-filled." The order sounded like a checklist being shouted out in a war zone. Fast. Precise. Clipped. The older woman behind the counter sensed her urgency and began to move back and forth quickly, rustling wax paper and folding flat cardboard into a box.

Mary Ann stepped to the left and said, "And today is special. Today is a 'Me Day' so I'm breaking into the Fancies." She smiled wide: "Put 1 Maple Frosted Coffee Roll and a Chocolate Iced Bismarck in there and let's round out the dozen."

The Dunkin Donuts employee hurried even faster, trying to remember the donut and Fancies order of a woman who spoke about donuts with complete authority. Some long haul truckers could do it, a half-dozen or so career secretaries could too. It was a point of pride for the older woman to not ask the younger woman to repeat her order.

Box in hand Mary Ann left the store thinking about how much joy she could buy for so little money. Eight dollars. Nothing that cost so little had ever made her so happy and for so long.

She tossed the box onto the drivers seat, sat down behind the wheel and said to the windshield, "Yup, boys. Mama's back."

She reached over to the box, ran a fingernail through the clear tape on each side of the lid and flipped it open. Inside was all sugary symmetry: It never failed to delight. All lined up and cozy in their box home, the donuts sat there, a perfect world waiting just for her.

"I.Want.You." she said to confectioner's sugar- covered jelly donut as she captured it between two fingers and pinched it from the box.

Holding the donut aloft, she put the car in reverse and backed out. Had anyone been watching, they would have seen her take a huge bite of a donut before turning the wheel in the opposite direction. As the car shot from the parking lot, they would have seen the driver flip her long blonde hair and lick white powder from her upper lip.

◼

A stonewall rose on one side of the car and pasture land rolled away from the other as she drove fast, listening to Springsteen. She went to see The Rising tour with Jair: He'd had one beer too many and ground his hips into her back during *She's the One*. Her fingers instinctively curled around the Chocolate Bismarck. The frosting was cool and slick beneath her fingers. It even feels good, she thought.

Air and light blew through her car. The faster she went, the further away from cars and people and obsession and drama she was. Out here, there was no talking about hair. There were no family budgets or forms or waiting rooms. Out here, Mary Ann thought, no one can get at me and I can think and feel and do and eat as I want. Out here, she realized, there was no Jair.

She was approaching the intersection. Her mind was locked in middle-aged rebelliousness when a flash of bright blue registered. It wasn't sky; it was darker and shinier. She slid the tip of the Bismarck into her mouth as she looked right. Springsteen was singing about driving through the Holland tunnel with a stolen radio he was gonna sell and then just throw that money on the bed.

Now that was a hot man, she thought, as her windshield turned completely blue. She braked hard. Had the sky fallen? Was this the Rapture?

No, it was a van. It was a huge blue van and it was turning. She saw white letters the size of her head, "La Iglesia…" turning right into the spot where her car would be in one second.

THWAMP! SCREEEEE.

The first point of contact between van and Camry bumper sent her teeth down hard upon each other. She tasted sugar and metal, most likely the tin of blood. Her eyes widened, bringing in more light and color. She noticed a huge clod of dirt that had come to rest by the road, roots and grass still attached. Hyper-aware and out of control, Mary Ann realized she was having a car wreck.

Her bumper was hooked just beneath the higher bumper of the van. As the two vehicles, now joined, continued to move down the country road, the sound of steel dragging on asphalt filled her brain. The noise bounced inside her skull as if she were smack in the middle of Rendition and about to crack to the Allies. Some piece of metal had come loose, hit the ground, and sent sparks flying.

She heard herself scream NOOOOO as she pulled the wheel hard to the right, hoping the butterfly lifts and Arnolds in the gym had given her upper arm strength. The effort brought her almost completely out of her seat and the endless SCREEEEE... finally stopped.

The Camry slipped beneath the van fender and popped out, another THWAMP! that completely filled and would later echo through Mary Ann's bones. That horrible sound! Dust shot out in all directions.

She punched the brakes hard and her car came to a stop. The last Bismarck crumbs had fallen to the passenger seat floor. Bits of car carpet clung to the icing.

She watched the back of the blue van get smaller and roll to a stop about 200 feet further down the road. There was no movement and no sound. She sat and listened to her own heartbeat.

That pastry might be salvageable, she thought.

Just a small chocolate loss. She looked up and noticed the glove compartment and thought she might need to get some papers from there. Then her eyes rose above the dashboard and her heartbeat ceased.

Two doors on both sides of the van were open and small brown men were stepping out onto the road. The back of the van was open too and she watched two more men climb out, side by side, and stand together. Another man came out of the left front door and she was sure at least four men had just stepped out of the other side. She started to count the men and had to recount as more joined the group milling around on the gravel.

Mary Ann started dialing frantically, touching the names of those she loved most, those who would help her during a life-threatening situation. She touched her husband's name, her son's. No one picked up. She tried the Palmers. No one. Her life had been so worry-free up to this moment, she really had no idea of how to even report a crime to the police. What am I reporting? she thought, too many brown men in one van? Oh yeah, the car, Mary Ann thought.

She pulled the door handle open. She sat in her Camry and stared at the van, hands shielding her eyes from sun. The words on the side of the van said, "La Igelsia del Redentor." What did that mean? She'd been bumped around, surprised, and woozy from too much sugar.

One of the small brown men worked his way to the front of the group standing around the van and shouted, "La mujer! La mujer! Esta bien?"

She didn't answer and he started to wave. She couldn't imagine what he wanted. Was he calling to her or about her? She didn't know.

Two of the men started walking towards the Camry's final resting spot. More began to follow. Mary Ann tried to think and could not. Old CNN reports, fuzzy and violent, began to play in her head.

In her mind, she could have been on the Arizona-Mexican frontier, fighting for her life. Where were those cartels? Los Angeles? New York? Where else?

Am I going to sit here until they shatter the glass and kill me? She jumped out of the car, hit the automatic lock button, and took off in the opposite direction, race-walking so fast the fat under her upper arms flapped.

◼

A quarter mile south, a 1978 yellow Cadillac with a white rag roof was moving down the rural two-lane at 75 miles an hour. Inside the car, the Philly R&B band Blue Magic was singing Chasing Rainbows.

Jay was at the wheel. He loved that smooth 70s shit, the music, the moves, the clothes. His ties were always wide to match his wide lapels that always laid flat. Today, long floral collars pointed out from underneath his brown jacket.

Jay's forefinger, ring finger, and pinky sparked with light off his diamonds as he moved his hands from the wheel to his lap and back again. His hair was slicked back into a ponytail held at the nape of his neck. Every few minutes, his tongue darted out to a half-open, half-closed wound on his lower lip.

Jay had carried his burden and stepped in during an attack on a homie. The homie lived and Jay left a piece of his lip and two front teeth in the mouth of the attacker.

In the seat next to him, Dashaun was playing with one of his wifeys, the legendary Peggy Sue. His favorite Peggy Sue had done so much damage, his homies had her image tattooed on their bodies. With her cute snub nose, Dashaun thought, every banger in the sett had finger fucked this bitch. She was his favorite wifey, a reliable hood whore, and she went wherever he did and did whatever he wanted to do every damn time he wanted to do it.

"Man why the fuck you got Peggy Sue out?" Jay asked.

"Why not? Who's gonna see," Dashaun answered as he rolled a few babies around in his hand. Peggy Sue had ten babies in her clip and one in her chamber. An extra bun in the oven for good luck, he often thought as he prepared to go to work nights. He and Jay and their long lost homie Reggie, AKA "Ragz." The three had been inseparable.

Every night they did work, Peggy Sue wailing away. Now it was just Dashaun and Jay. Ragz disappeared and they were young two men, stepping around the huge bloody wound where Ragz once stood. The two were still banging away without him, but they were family men now, more cautious, older, men with children and wives.

"Ain't nobody gonna see," Dashaun repeated. "Like some bear gonna take it off me."

"Trillz," Jay said as he squinted at the road ahead of him. Dashaun was his business partner. They had grown up on the streets together, gone to college together. By day, Dashaun had been the all-American boy, a promising NBA draft, and a big man on campus. Girls loved the look of his long dreads, chinky eyes, and coiled muscle. His volatility attracted and repelled in equal measure.

He was the first one into battle and then came springing back out over the bodies, acrid-smoke hanging in the air. He was like an avenging ghost jumping back through the fire. "No fear" didn't begin to describe it. The history of every injustice ever committed against a black man still lived in Dashaun. Any threat could set it loose. Once loose, people died.

"…just giving mah old lady a shine…." Dashaun said as he looked back up from his lap and out the windshield.

"WHOA. What's that," he said.

◻

Jay and Dashaun stared at the road ahead. A tall blonde was coming toward them fast, a dust cloud floating in the air behind her.

"WHOA. That's a white bitch," Jay said with awe. He'd run these roads for years and never saw anyone, no less some white lady in slacks with a cardigan billowing behind her, walking fast in the middle of absolutely nowhere.

"Yo man, go down the middle. Smoke her," Dashaun said.

"What the fuck 'smoke her'," Jay shot back. "She a white lady running. Or at least walking real fast."

"Man, we fucking CANNOT stop." What made Dashaun a great leader was his focus. The focus also made him a douche. He was all business.

"Well look at her!" Jay said. "And wad the fuck you mean I can't stop. It's my fucking car. Can't stop. That some shit. You sitting there with Peggy Sue and you afraid of a white woman swinging a purse?"

"We ain't doing this shit," Dashaun repeated. "It's my car."

"Yeah, your car. But I got Peggy Sue and we're not fucking stopping. We got business, a deadline, people waiting on the other end. Man we got no time for this shit here." Dashaun was already fingering the wifey, his beloved Peggy Sue.

"We can't leave some white lady in the middle of nowhere," Jay said.

"Shit we can. White lady? FUCK HER especially."

Mary Ann was closer and they could see her features clearly. A streaky redness had settled on her puffed up cheeks. Her brown eyes glistened with exertion and fear and streaks of tearstains bisected the dust beneath her eyes. She walked with a strange sliding motion, as if her shoes were too large and about to fly off.

"She bright pink and gray! She in trouble," Jay said just as the first part of the scrum of small brown men in t-shirts and jeans appeared in the distance behind her. Arms waving, snippets of Spanish words were rising from them: Mujer!, Ayuda!, Parada!, No haremos!

"WHOA. Now what the fuck is that?" Dashaun had spotted the Mexicans and Jay knew what he would say next and he did: "Shit, Jay Mexicans never wanted to do anything but kill a nigga."

"They don't know we're here, D," came Jay's voice of reason. "Come on man, who we? She's out here alone. They gangbangers."

"No man! I told you! We have product here. They waiting for us on the other side. We ain't stopping for this bitch."

"Too many Mexicans for ya?"

"Fuck you, man." Jay knew that if he appealed to the warrior in Dashaun, he would relent. Being outnumbered was a life challenge Dashaun enjoyed a great deal.

Without further discussion, Jay floated the huge car to the far right side of the road and began to slow. Dashaun opened his car door and when they were along side the woman, Jay jerked the wheel and Dashaun reached out and pulled her onto his lap and closed the door. Jay hit the accelerator and the nose of the giant car rose up. He steered the car into the wrong lane in order to get around the Mexicans.

"What…what!...WHAT!...." the squirming white

woman was yelling. The Mexicans had come to a stop and stood staring open mouthed at the Caddy. They saw the woman and began to shout. Inside the Caddy, they heard Spanish words as they passed: Mujere! Pilagro! Negros!

Inside the Caddy, all three passengers stared at the Mexicans. Dashaun, Jay and Mary Ann read "La Iglesia del Redentor" and "Catolicos" on their t-shirts and on the back of the van.

"...who...are...." Mary Ann spoke into her twisted cardigan as she tried to get it off her body.

"Yo, Lady. Sit." Dashaun snapped as he tightened one arm around her and slid her between them on the long bench of the 1970s front car seat.

Her head was swiveling wildly. Her mouth would not work at all. She looked at one man then the other then back at the first man. There were two, she knew that much. She was in a car with two men. Two black men. Was this as or more dangerous than the twelve Mexican men outside?

"What.The.Fuck...." Jay said, looking at Mary Ann. "We just saved yo ass from a church van?"

■

"I told you, man. I told you not to stop." Dashaun had his arm on Mary Ann and was glaring at Jay. "I told you. Now, we late."

"I thought you knew Spanish, motherfucker. You

had that hot Dominican piece on the side all those years. How the fuck you not know that a church?" Jay demanded.

"I didn't 'talk' to her like that nigga and I most certainly didn't go to church with her hot high ass," Dashaun said. "And who you looking at like that, Mr. Bilateral?"

"Bilingual," Mary Ann croaked.

"Oh fuck. We got us a school marm! She gonna correct our grammar!" Dashaun said.

"Ma'am," Jay said. "Where do you need to go?"

"...ah....I....," she was staring at the wound on Jay's lower lip. Her mouth was moving but no real words formed.

"A gas station? Will that help? "

"Yes, yes it would," she managed to say. Then to Dashaun, "can you let go?"

"Fuck yeah, I'd love to let go but no shit 'til we get you to Exxon."

"It doesn't have to be an Exxon," she croaked.

"I know that!" Dashaun exploded inside the car.

Jay glanced at him and smiled. Here we go, he thought. "I know that! We stopped for a fucking white bitch! Makes no fuckin' sense, man. Shut up!"

When he was this mad, vibrations pulsated outward and the sensation was not pleasant. It was an energy that either frightened a homie or energized him. If Dashaun sensed weakness, a dude was gone. If a dude wanted to be Dashaun, he better be as tough.

Posers were dispatched quickly.

"…I would appreciate you not calling me that again…" She looked more surprised than either man that she'd gotten so many words out.

Jay touched the knob on the car stereo and Blue Magic's *What's Come Over Me* was all over the cavernous inside of the Cadillac. Dashaun grimaced and looked at Jay. Jay smiled and looked at Mary Ann. She looked out the front window, staring half into the rear view mirror and half onto the road. Her face was covered in beige dust save those two clear streaks beneath each eye. That white bitch comment must have hurt, Jay thought.

"Call you what? White bitch?" Dashaun's voice was a bit higher than normal, a mock-offended tone, Jay supposed. "Ha!" He turned and stared out the side window.

Her "me time" had turned to shit in a second. All she had wanted was a fast drive with something delicious to eat. Alone. She just wanted an hour. One hour. Was it too much to ask?

"Don't mind him," Jay said. "He forget his manners." He leaned forward, took his eyes off the long straight road and fixed eyes with Dashaun, "And you, nigga. Since when don't you like white women? My. My. Not what I heard." He smiled, turning on the electricity inside the car.

Mary Ann sat between them, neck strained back so as not to disrupt the sightline of these two male lions sniffing around each other's territory.

"I don't recall saying I didn't like to spin the white bitches, I just don't want to drive they asses around," Dashaun replied.

"Can you wait to discuss the sexual merits of white women until after you leave me at the Exxon?" Mary Ann asked.

"It doesn't have to be an Exxon," Dashaun said.

"I know that!" Mary Ann exploded over the crooning Blue Magic.

What a love couple, Jay thought as he smiled through the windshield. Dashaun and women: Anger fueled every attraction. Nothing was sexier to women, Jay mused, than a man barely in check. Jay used the move himself, again and again. He glanced at the two, silent and closed. All three still heard Mary Ann's "I know that!" pinging around the cavernous car.

Mary Ann realized the moment was her bottom, a personal "low." Her husband only talked about his own hair. She was a bald guy's Mommy and it made her skin creep. Always on edge, she was constantly looking at young men and was afraid she might inadvertently growl at one of them, perhaps one of her son's friends. The thought filled her with shame. She was teetering on the abyss. Eating and driving had led to a wrecked car, race walking and black men. That's what you get, Mary Ann Carlyle, she thought, for not being mistress of your own damn domain.

With new clarity, her feelings turned dark. What a

shit life, she thought. While her son and husband were off living their lives, she had locked herself inside one of America's most popular cars with a dozen donuts and started to eat and drive.

The moment was profound. Mary Ann saw her reactions to the shit of her life, and she didn't like it. The car, the donuts, the disgust, the boredom, the fear. What she couldn't know was more shit was on the way. This shit? The Mexicans? These black guys in the Caddy? This here was just some more for the pile of annoying shit. Tragic, epic crap would arrive later.

And unbeknownst to Mary Ann, that epic crap was already hurtling toward her via a route so old, no one even noticed it anymore.

Within days, the U.S. Postal Service would innocently slip an envelope in the mailbox by the front door. It would land on her floor without a sound.

The blast would come later, when she opened it.

◘

Inside the car, no one said a word. She turned her head slightly to the left and looked at Jay. He had more diamonds than Lillith Glassman, and she had a lot. He was staring out at the road, humming along to the R&B. She turned her head slightly to the right, and Dashaun was glaring back at her, two green chunky-looking green eyes filled with distrust and disgust.

"I want to thank you," she said. "My husband has just had surgery and I'm under a lot of stress. I panicked there for a second." Then she let out a polite little flat grocery store laugh.

"I just had surgery," Jay said.

"What kind," she said, relieved to have a topic.

"Motherfucker bit Jay's mouth off. Took two teeth."

"Motherfucker," Dashaun spat.

Jay smiled and said, "What kind of surgery did your husband have?"

"He had 1500 hairs transplanted. Hair restoration surgery. He's going bald."

"Wha.....a...a?" Dashaun exploded. "Yo! HAIR SURGERY. We fucking picked up a white bitch married to a no hair! What the fuck! Yo! JAY! What we doin', Man?" He laughed and flipped his shoulder-blade length dreads. Unconsciously, Jay's diamond ringed fingers reached for his ponytail as he smiled.

"It was very important for his self-esteem," she said.

"Self-esteem!" The words exploded in the car. "I got me some self and some esteem," Jay said, fumbling with his pants zipper.

"Ain't you talking about looking in the da mirror and shit?" Dashaun asked.

"It's like I said, Man, crazy white people. They call staring in the mirror 'self-esteem' to act like it's something besides more selfish bullshit. Crazy white people. Crazy white bitch."

She turned to Jay and said, "I'm taking offense at how many times he's called me 'white bitch'."

Jay smiled. "You are funny. For a white woman in a car with two niggas you don't know." He turned the wheel in one smooth motion, flashes of light playing off his rings playing inside the car.

"Oh, believe me," she said, eyes flooded and glowing. "The ni..ni...nigga part has not eluded me."

Jay threw his head back and laughed, rings and teeth flashing.

Just three minutes before, she'd been running, completely alone, from a vanload of religious Mexicans. Now, two black men half her age were about to drop her at a gas station at the strip malls on the edge of town. So heady was the action, she realized she'd left the donuts to grow stale and hard in the passenger's seat of her Camry.

"Here we go," Jay said as he floated the car into the first gas station he saw, the Gas N' Go on Empire Street.

Dashaun jumped out of the car and held the door open, glaring. She scooted toward him across the long bench of the '73 Caddy and saw his fire-engine red high- topped Chuck Taylors. Interesting color, she thought as she made a great show of going around him. She walked to the driver's side.

Jay rolled down his window as she took out her wallet and extracted a card.

"I can't thank you enough," she said. "Here's my

card. Please, if I can ever help you...."

The whole gesture was a joke, she thought as she turned and walked away from the men. How could she ever return a favor to two people who could take anything they wanted?

Jay looked at the card, reached forward and grabbed a pen from the detritus in his car caddy jammed beneath the stereo. Mary Ann Carlyle, it said. Then, so as to remind himself later who she was, he scrawled "HAIR" in big letters across her name.

◾

Walking into his apartment, Jay led carrying the bag. Dashaun was two steps behind, Peggy Sue in his waistband. This was where Jay lived with his girlfriend and their two children, all of whom he sent to her Mom's house for the breakdown.

The breakdown was Jay and Dashaun's favorite part. They had paid the Italian, met the plane, unloaded the shit and gotten it home with nothing but a brief encounter with a white woman. This job was easy.

Other runs had sucked lately. They had endless hours of discussion about getting older, raising kids. Take off the tatts and red rags and, based on their conversation topic, these two could have been any two dudes on Metro North from Manhattan. Patios, wives, in-laws, kids, the money squeeze, tuition.

Jay took off his jacket and put it on the back of a

chair at the dining room table. Piled high with saran wrap and self-sealing baggies, this table was where Jay fed his babies and broke down dope. Dashaun and he would sit there, breaking it down into six smaller packages while drinking and yelling at the television. They'd be happy, thinking about getting paid. Six smaller packages would then be wrapped in many layers of plastic wrap. This much weed in one place left skunk smell on everything. Febreze helped.

"Bro, when you ordering the fucking pizza. I'm hungry," Jay said.

"Shut up. I ordered it already from the car and we going to pick it up so we can stop at the liquor store."

"Oh hell yeah, nigga," Jay said. "I hope you didn't order that dumb ass cheese crust shit."

"Fuck you nigga that shit is good," Dashaun laughed as he walked to the door.

"I'm not paying for that pizza," Jay followed. "Why not?" Dashaun asked.

"That shit's for two year olds," Jay said as he locked the door behind them and headed back to the car.

"Whatever man. That shit is da bomb," Dashaun said, looking in every direction as they left the apartment.

"Let's grab the food and drinks 'cuz I don't want to be baggin' all night," Jay backed the 1973 Cadillac out of his large secret parking space and onto Lenox Avenue. The car reeked of unburned weed.

"Yo man, this car stinks. How'd that white bitch

not smell it," Dashaun said as he settled in. He looked at Jay. "She probably thought she smelled some kinda MULCH or some shit." His shoulders began to shake. "Dude!" Dashaun was really laughing, his eyes slits, nostrils flaring. "She probably smell that shit and think we gardeners of somethin'." He was rocking forward and back into his seat. "Lemon verbena. Black man potpourri. Oh man, that some funny." He looked at Jay staring at the road, the edges of his smiled curled up into Joker territory. "Nigga, why you got that stupid ass smirk on your face?"

Jay laughed. "Nothing," he replied.

"I know your ass is thinking 'bout your new charity, Save the White Bitch," Dashaun said.

"Damn, D," Jay turned the wheel left. "That some real racist shit, Nigga. But she did have a nice ass. And those legs, Man. I felt 'em wrapped around my neck, pumping away." His smile split his face in half and made his sore lip throb.

"I knew it. I KNEW IT! You ass stop for this bitch 'cuz you want to fuck her."

"Bro," Jay shot back, "the dumbest shit come out your mouth."

"Nigga, DO NOT tell me your two exchanged phone numbers," Dashaun said, glaring out the window now.

■

Jay floated the Caddy into its hiding spot behind the dumpster, two Stuff-Crusted Pan Pizzas, a bottle of Gran Marnier XO, two 40 ounce bottles of Colt 45 and two 24-ounce bottles of Olde English in the back seat.

Jay liked the way cognac slid down his throat, painting his insides. Dashaun craved cheap old school beer. He'd always smile after a huge pull and say "mother's milk."

Jay suspected D had picked it up from his Dad.

"Some nigga die in there…" Dashaun said out the open car window.

"I know it, right?" Jay said as he picked up the pizza boxes. Dashaun had a huge bag of beer in one hand and fingers wrapped around the neck of the cognac. "Smells like that all day everyday," Jay said. "I think those Caribbean motherfuckers that own that restaurant use it. Not supposed to."

Before either man moved again, Dashaun said, "Bro, the family's not supposed to be back yet, is they?" His tone was low and flat.

Jay looked to the left. "Fuck no, that's not she car," he said. He could hear Dashaun cock the .38. Jay was now relieved Dashaun had spent the run diddling around with Peggy Sue. "But that's where she usually park it."

"Get your gun ready, Bro. Circle the complex," Dashaun said. Immediately, Jay's left hand went to the wifey under the seat as his right hand yanked the car into reverse.

The two men did a slow circle around the apartments. Doors were closed and nothing moved. They turned a corner slowly and when they passed directly in front of Jay's house, a door exploded open and three dudes came running out hard. Across the street, an SUV shot out of nowhere to pick the three up.

Jay slammed on the brakes, threw the car into park, and both men jumped out of the Cadillac.

"Get the house! I got the car!" Jay yelled as he ran towards the front door. Dashaun charged the SUV, dreads flying loose, gun drawn.

POP! POP! POP! Jay heard Dashaun working behind him, shooting through the car's windows at the frantic men inside. POP! POP! POP! Jay couldn't quite figure why he didn't hear return fire. POP!

Beside the door, Jay peered into his house. This was a feeling he knew well. Fury and nervousness fought inside him: Anything moves, it'll die. He heard a car engine roar behind him. In seconds, Dashaun was next to him, breathing hard. No more than 90 seconds had passed.

"You hit anything, Bro?" Jay whispered. "Aired the car out. Three motherfuckers. Don't know if anyone in the house." His chest was rising and falling. The qualities that had made Dashaun a basketball hero all counted on the street: speed, strength, fearlessness, domination, jumping.

"Shit man, if they in here, they ain't getting out alive."

■

Jay raised his gun and sucked in a chest-full of air. He looked at Dashaun. Dashaun looked back and nodded. They had done this so many times it was almost involuntary, a nerve ending jumping from heat.

As the door swung open, the two men took one step into the house, guns up and ready, every cell alert and moving faster, heads clear. Jay's gun pointed to the left side of the living room. Dashaun focused on the dining room table and the bar that separated living area from kitchen.

A confused look overtook Dashaun. He cocked his head to one side and stood there for several breaths. He turned to Jay and whispered, "you hear that?"

Jay, walking on the far side of the apartment, stopped. "What the fuck you doin', man?"

'Shut up," Dashaun hissed. He paused and his voice softened, "it's a lil' nigga cryin'."

Jay's face loosened as his focus broke. Dashaun pointed Peggy Sue at the swinging door into the kitchen. He gestured toward Jay to come to the door. Again, they assumed the position just as they had at the front door. Jay stood on one side as Dashaun slowly pushed it open. Anything moved, they'd fire.

Jay stepped into the half-open door and saw a small form on the floor. Balled up and mumbling "don't shoot, don't shoot," the little pile of clothes on the floor was alive and begging.

Jay stood over the boy glaring while Dashaun bent to untangle him.

"This little fucker here? THIS LITTLE FUCKER HERE?" Jay's rage boiled back up and over. "All this shit is for this little pile of fuck here?" he repeated.

This little fuck was in the house where his children sleep. Where their Mother made their meals. This little bit of fuck had brought the street into Jay's home.

"I say FUCK THIS LITTLE FUCKER RIGHT HERE," Jay screamed before he pulled the trigger.

Pop! The bullet caught the kid in beef of his upper arm, twisting him left into the cabinet.

A high-pitched "GAH!" filled the room. Jay leapt to the tiny pile now jammed in the far corner by the stove. He grabbed a handful of shirt, pulled the kid's head back, and stared into his face. Dashaun reached for Jay just as he brought the barrel of the gun up to the small snot-encrusted nose.

"I sorry! I sorry!" the ball cried harder.

"Fuck you and the mother that birth you," Jay said quietly, straight into the kid's face as he began to squeeze the trigger.

"Nigga! NIGGA! What's this new shit?" Dashaun edged his body between Jay and the kid. He grabbed Jay's gun by the barrel and said, "What the fuck got into you, Man? This a kid."

"Nigga," Jay says as he steps back, "are you for real? This kid here fucking with grown men. This kid here fucking with everything I have. Everything I do."

Dashaun just kept staring. "What, Nigga. Stop looking like that. Go find church somewhere," Jay said as he turned away.

"Stop buggin', bro and look at his face. He a kid." "Nigga, this is looking like a bad scene from Pulp Fiction. What's your point? Because you gotta give me one good reason to not open up this little nigga's face," Jay said as he moved back to the little pile. He caught the tip of his shoe on the kid's leg and said, "I'm a gonna fuck your little face up so you Mommy can't kiss you goodbye." Another whimper filled the room, more for the reminder of his home life than the thought of blood oozing down his side.

Dashaun put his hand on the boys arm. The whimpering stopped. He shook his head, looked up at the ceiling, then back at Jay.

"Don't forget where we come from, Man. We did this same shit all the time. You feel you different because we never got caught. Could be us, Man. This little kid. "

Jay stood silent, face changing as he thought this through. Dashaun pulled the boy to his feet. He walked him to the sink. The kid didn't make a sound. He peeled off his little sweater and whistled as he opened the bloody shirt.

Jay watched as Dashaun began to clean the boy's wound. So much blood.

He found his temper rising again and said,"...all this from a man who didn't want to help a white bitch. Get this bleeding motherfucker out my kitchen before

I change my mind."

"Bro, can I at least have a towel for him?" Dashaun asked as he continued to examine the kid's wound.

"Fuck him. Damn lil' nigga. This little motherfucker tracking blood and mud all over my house. Why you don't let him drip on the kids' toys? Shit, get this fool a maxi pad to catch that blood and take his dirty ass boots out my house."

◘

Jay heard the tub running. He had sat down on the couch, still furious. Dashaun and the kid had moved from the kitchen to the bathroom and he hadn't even seen them go by.

Jay got up off the couch, walked to the doorway and said, "Bro, you need to figure out what to do with your little pet. Cause his ass is not staying or dying here."

Jay had had a gut of it, this constant state of siege. The kid disgusted him. He had started banging at sixteen, Dashaun had been twelve. But they'd never been this stupid, despite what D said. They'd never disrespected an OG like this kid had disrespected him.

Dashaun had the kid naked from the waist up and was wiping blood from his chest with an old towel Jay had finally given up.

"You one funny-ass nigga," Dashaun said over the kid towards Jay. "You would help some white bitch who doesn't give a flying fuck about you but this kid. This kid has lost his way; you ready to kill him."

"You damn right," Jay fired back. "No white people trying to rob me. It's dumb ass kids like this. Fuck we all lost, Nigga. But robbin' our asses? Shit. Some of us make it; some of us have to die. We didn't birth this boy and we don't owe him shit."

"No white people trying to rob you and only thing a cop care about is you killing whitey. Pigs don't even come if you shoot a lil' nigga like this so shut the fuck up with your dumb crime shit and help me," Dashaun said. 'We lucky we found him. Cops would have dumped him with the Crabs and let him bleed out. Run the tub so I can clean the hole you made."

The kid was small, just under 5 feet. He'd lost a lot of blood and was docile, his huge black wet eyes following the two men as they argued his fate. He didn't know how he got separated from the others. They were picking up the dope and he thought about a computer. He started looking around the apartment for one. Or an iPod. He had just had a birthday and he wanted — deserved — a fucking present. He was looking for one when Jay and Dashaun drove up.

Dashaun wiped the kid's arm and back. "Bro, come check it out" he said to Jay. "Look at his tatts."

Jay stepped to the tub. He looked at the tatt Dashaun had stretched tight under his thumb and forefinger. Jay's eyes grew wide. He looked like he'd seen a ghost.

He stepped back and said to the kid, "where the fuck you get dat tatt?"

The blood-smeared tattoo was a bull with a man's head. Horns protruded and fire shot from the nose. Jay had sketched it out and gotten the first one. His sett followed. Jay had never seen this kid before. How'd he get this tatt?

The kid looked back, eyes lit for the first time. He said nothing.

"Let's try again," Jay said as he leaned over the tub. "Where da fuck did you get that tatt? Better yet, who gave it to you? Speak little nigga or you dying in this tub." The kid stared back and started to wiggle as Dashaun continued to wipe blood off him.

"Oh, you must think I have a heart today," Dashaun said to the kid. "You ass still have to answer for this shit. Chill or I'll let my homeboy deal with you and you don't want that."

The kid stopped moving save where his heart was pounding against the wall of his chest.

"This kid comes from inside your sett, Bro. That's the only way to explain the tatt," Dashaun said.

Jay's throat closed. "I need water. You want a cup?" he croaked.

"Yeah."

While Jay walked to the kitchen, he heard Dashaun repeating over and over "do you know who my homeboy is? You know who my homeboy is?"

Jay filled two glasses with water and walked back to

the bathroom. He handed a glass to Dashaun. Both men drank deeply then looked back at the boy in the tub.

"Yo, man," Dashaun said to Jay, "niggas set you up. We'll get the info we need now. I'll get it from the kid. We'll handle them."

Jay turned, walked out of the bathroom and went back to sit on the couch.

◼

Mary Ann swung the Camry in behind Jair's Lexus. He's home early, she thought as she balled up trash off the passenger seat. She walked past the front window and could see Jair's head bobbing to and fro in the kitchen. Two weeks post-hair restoration surgery, he looked like an action hero from the neck up, all stubble and scab. Below, he was still a roly-poly American guy who went from football to fat in his third decade.

She stepped onto the front porch and in one smooth arc picked the mail off the ground as she slid the key in the lock. Nobody notices the middle-aged suburban ballerina, she thought as she pushed the door open and threw the mail on the side table. Nobody.

Mary Ann walked the hall and into the light of the kitchen. Jair had moved. She looked out the kitchen window and could see him out back, standing in brown leaves and gesturing. His crooked elbow informed her he had a phone to his head. Used to be, men got bad elbows from lifting beers. Now this. This jabbering. Cellphones clutched like a lucky rabbit's foot in the hands of her husband and son. Day in. Day out. Everyone was always talking in this house, she thought, just never to me.

She walked to the sliding glass door that Jair left open. She opened her mouth to call his name and stopped. Something about his body language was off.

She couldn't see his face. One hand held the phone and the other hand was on his hip. He had turned his right leg outward and appeared to be snuffing out a cigarette with the toe of an orange New Balance running shoe.

There was no cigarette, just the strange movement. For a second, she imagined Jair in a canopied bed, pink Princess phone at his head. She shook it off.

She turned and went in the kitchen and stood behind the sink. She could still see all of Jair out of the window. He seemed to need so much, she thought. So much attention and care. She hadn't counted on that.

When she'd taken over paying the family's expenses, she observed his need through his spending. In the early years, it was all Home Depot and groceries. Then it was the ever-enlarging flat screens escalating into Donna Karan and cresting at the Lexus dealership. Throughout, he continued to lecture her about money and waste.

His son, now his height, seemed to confuse him. Jair would stand back looking at her and Jeremy with a bemused look on his face. The kid needed clothes, gadgets, lots of food. Jair would bargain with him, offering to give him his old phone when the contract was up.

No go, the kid would say, I want my own, not your used crap. And the war was on. She'd look at her son. Then she'd look at Jair and say, "You know, you invited us here. We just didn't crawl in through the doggie door like common raccoons."

She kept staring, still entranced by her husband's coy stance. She wondered who was on his phone, getting him to look all girly. She quickly ruled out Peter, though he had the butt of a woman. A colleague? Well, that didn't seem likely. He thought they were bores. No, it wasn't one of them. This was something else.

She saw the brown leaves lift a bit off the ground around Jair's feet. God knows wind wouldn't ruffle his hair, she thought. He finished up the conversation with a skyward fist, then took the phone from his head and ended the call. He stood for a moment looking straight ahead.

Then he turned toward the house and Mary Ann suddenly saw it all.

Beneath a cut, swollen head, Jair's eyes were shining like a possum in headlights, still hanging from the garbage can. His lips were shiny from the excited nervous licking she knew so well. It couldn't be the hair people; he saw them earlier today. His body language was light, as if he weighed 50 pounds less and he was even wearing his khaki shorts.

As he took a step towards the house, she felt her stomach clench. Acid and adrenaline flooded her system. She felt cold. Don't come in here, you fat motherfucker, she thought. All the time and the money and the cooing and the cooking and the fetching. Her ribs ached and she pulled at the air in the kitchen trying to get enough to fill her lungs.

That fat motherfucker, she thought.

With the shiny eyes and moist pie hole, he might has well have taken out an ad. She knew what was going on now. It hadn't been hair restoration that had triggered that old shiny-eyed, moist-lipped look. And it certainly hadn't been her.

That fat motherfucker, she thought. That fat fucker was getting laid.

◘

"These taste like candy, Hon!" Jair said as he speared another Brussels sprout sautéed in brown butter.

She didn't remember preparing the meal. She didn't remember her son coming home and setting the table. But here they were, a family eating dinner.

"Candy, huh?" she said. "Found some wrappers in the Lexus, Daddy-O."

"Wha..." Jair said as he looked up from the half-Brussels impaled on his fork. "What? Oh, ha. Yes, the flesh is weak. I want to show you the new decoy I bought. It's already shelved. A vintage canvasback by

Scott Johnson. The paint is glorious! The most popular, the best."

"The best, Jair? Hardly. I found candy wrappers in your car. A lot of them." She looked down at her food and began sawing on her chicken breast. She knew full well that in marriage, lying, cheating, betraying, hiding, flaunting, swiping, spending, forgetting and snoring were all fair game. But here was something new: the overwhelming desire to tell her husband he's fat. This was very wrong and she knew it. It just swelled in her and pushed, creating an unbearable stress. If she didn't call him fat, she herself would expand until she blew apart. If she didn't call him fat, she would call him an adulterer in front of their son.

"Wha…What? What is that you say?" Jair looked alarmed. He was not used to such strange disrespect from Mary Ann.

"Yeah. Candy. You know, you put candy in your mouth. It goes in your body. You get fat."

"I…"

"You're fat, Jair. Not even enough room in those shorts of yours for a few Skittles." She could feel her insides give.

Jeremy choked, looked at his Mother, then his Father, then his plate. He was used to adult weirdness but this was new. He smiled.

"What's so funny, young man?" Jair boomed at his amused son.

"No….noth…" Jeremy was really laughing now.

"Fat as a pig stuffed into a khaki casing," Mary Ann said, unable to stop herself and no longer caring. "eating candy in a big SUV."

"You can't talk to me like that!" Jair shouted.

She couldn't stop: it was out on the table and running around.

"You're fat! You're fat! You're fat!" she shouted back. She knew it was childish and far from the point but it just felt so good to finally yell it at his fat ass. That fat motherfucker, she thought, having all that fun on the phone. Where's that flirtatious stance now, baldy?

Jair stood up quickly. His chair tipped back and hit the ground.

"I don't have to take this!" he yelled at Mary Ann and their son.

"That's it. Run, Fatty, run!" She could not believe what was coming out of her mouth. She would not have been able to stop it even if she tried. She had stood powerless for years as her husband walked around her like a useful appliance that dispensed ice. After twenty years of not seeing, she saw. The word "fat" seemed to make her giddy every time she said it and she wasn't going to stop now.

Jair left the room, leaving his chair sideways on the floor.

Jeremy stared at his Mother. Finally kid, she thought.

Finally, you notice me.

She looked into Jeremy's eyes and said, "guess he doesn't like candy after all."

She stood, walked out of the room, into the hall, took the pile of bills and went to her room.

Jeremy cleared the table with cellphone at his head, amusing his friends with tales of his Mother's rage. Most of his friends talked about their folks as if they were describing a show on the SyFy Channel. He finally had a story to throw on the pile.

Mary Ann could still hear Jeremy banging dinner dishes as she carried the mail into her room and sat down. Her internal pressure eased somewhat. Her ears buzzed a little and she felt drunk. She picked up a mechanical pencil and sliced the first bill open with the tip. There I was, she thought, not having sex with young men because of my fat husband.

She looked down and saw it was a routine cable bill.

She picked up the next envelope, ground the tip of the pencil into the envelope flap, and pulled it apart. I have been married all these years, she thought, almost twenty, and only went up a size. Her stomach began to clench again. She pulled the bill out, a huge one from Jeremy's school, and put it on top of the cable bill.

I've gone all these years without an engagement ring, she thought. Look at that fat fucker with his ducks. Sell a couple and buy me a nice ring. But no, that never crossed his mind. She picked up the next envelope and saw it was the MasterCard statement.

This one will mess me up, Mary Ann thought. This one's gonna be a whale. She dug the flap up with her pencil and sliced the bill open. Whoever was talking to Jair on the phone will need lots of money to maintain his head. Yup, that bitch will get lots of bills like this.

She unfolded the papers. She sighed, knowing she was at a big ending. She hadn't seen this shit coming.

She hadn't been watching. As her husband got fatter and more obsessed, she hadn't imagined anyone would actually want him. She found Jair so nonsexual she could not longer imagine that anyone else could see him as a sexual being either.

She was wrong. She'd convinced herself that's why she didn't stick her tail in the air like the cougar she'd dreamed of being. Mary Ann realized she hadn't just "settled" for Jair, she had actually become his pimp and his patsy.

On her next inhale, she looked down at the page, eyes searching for the bolded number. I can't just keep going without grown-up love, without appreciation, without sex, she thought. Real sex, like she watched on her iPad.

Her eyes saw the dark ink and locked on, a tremor beginning in the backs of her legs.

That fat fucker, she thought.

She read $24,132.00 and her middle American, middle-aged mind went black.

■

She had no memory of moving to the computer. She was freezing and had started to shake. The familiar sound of her machine grabbing hold of the ether brought the room back in focus.

She sat down as mail filled her homepage. All of it was spam. At the top of her inbox, an email from the Hair Loss Learning Center caught her eye. Her hand moved to the mouse and clicked:

BALDNESS CURE COULD BE ON SHELVES IN TWO YEARS

Researchers have isolated the single enzyme, called prostaglandin D2 (PGD2), responsible for hair loss.

George Cotsarelis, head of dermatology at Pennsylvania University, is now in talks with several drug firms about creating the anti-balding product...

She looked away from the computer. She wasn't thinking about what she read, she was feeling it. Every muscle in her body tensed as it all washed over her. Lies. Infidelity. Baldness. Betrayal.

She typed in Yahoo and clicked on mail. What would that fat fucker have used for a password she wondered. She entered her own name. Refused. She typed in the name of his favorite decoy artist: Elmer Crowell, master of the Canadian goose. Refused. She typed her son's name: Jeremy. Then she read the tiny writing on the screen requiring a capital letter, 6 characters and a number. She knew how the fat man's mind worked and typed in their son's name and age: Jeremy16.

She was in. Fuck you, fat boy! She thought as she began scrolling through his inbox. She found what she was looking for: Carilee at Yahoo.

She clicked on a random email:

> **Jair**: The doc said pool water won't affect my new hair.
>
> **Carilee**: We can go swimming.
>
> **Jair**: Forget swimming! I'm getting you against a hot tub jet.
>
> She clicked again:
>
> **Carilee**: I don't think I should be with the boss, it's just not right.
>
> **Jair**: I'm not the boss. You're the boss. And you know it.

She clicked again:

> **Carilee**: I like the way the seats go back in the Camry....

Mary Ann began to scroll, open, read, print. Scroll, open, read, print. Words jumped out at her over and over:

LOVE TOUCH PINK HAIR TOUCH TOGETHER LOVE SEXY THIGHS FAST TELL TELL OFFICE TELL KISS CAMRY SECRET HAIR WIFE HUSBAND SON TELL TELL SOFT TELL HAIR HARD TELL COCK TELL CAMRY TELL LIPS MOUTH TELL

She read every single email between Jair and his bald-loving mistress. Carilee was very young and working for the first time at her first job out of college.

She was Jair's assistant and she was deeply in love. With him.

She soon had 15 emails from Carilee printed and stacked. She felt it a good "best of" collection. She stood up.

She knew what to do now. She reached forward and extracted a paper clip from the "Hello, Florida!" shot glass on her desk. She slid it onto the stack of emails from Carilee. It's a slick presentation, she thought as she turned and walked slowly toward her clueless husband, watching T.V. and fingering the clicker in The Duck Room.

◼

Jair was watching a Jets game he'd recorded. She stood in the doorway taking him in. She understood this was the last time she'd see this. It was the last time anything would ever be like this.

"Hey," he said. "You here to see the newest duck?"

"No, Jair," she said quietly. "I'm not."

She walked to where he lay on the sofa, beady-eyes unmoving on shelves above him, and passed him the emails. He looked at the top one and looked up.

"Wha..?" he began. "Carilee."

The air changed and the room filled with the smell of old socks and underarms.

"You broke into my private email!" he shouted, jumping to his feet.

"Fat fucker!" she shouted. "You fucked Carilee in my Camry!"

"No! I didn't fuck her. I gave her a ride!"

"Fat jiggly fuck! With the seat down?????" Mary Ann screamed.

"I...I..." Jair was red in the face. He tried to do a back to front gesture, but his scalp was too sore. He winced and his hand went to his eyes and started rubbing.

"What? I...I...I....WHAT?" She had advanced and was almost standing on the toe of his orange running shoe.

"She...I...she..."

"She WHAT?" Mary Ann screamed, spittle hitting his chin.

He stopped rubbing and stared at her. The whites of his eyes were red and she could see down through his pupil all the way to bone. She saw space and ache and need. All his escalating ticks—the back to front head rubbing and ha-HANKING—were the hissing sound of fetid air seeking to escape from the insides of a cheat and a liar. It was the first time she had really seen her husband in years and she was horrified.

"She wants me, Mary Ann," he said with tears spilling down his face. "She makes me feel good."

"You. Fat. Fucker," she hissed into his wet face.

"You tricked me into getting your little whore hair and I will never forgive you. Now get the fuck out before I tell our son."

◼

Mary Ann returned to her room. She didn't know how much time had passed when she felt her son behind her. She turned.

"Mom," he said. "Dad's gone."

"Okay," she said.

"What happened?" Jeremy asked. "He has a girlfriend," Mary Ann said.

"WOW. WHOA. Wha...WHO?" Jeremy shot back.

"Don't know, Son," Mary Ann said as she stepped past him. "Someone named Carilee. She is his assistant. At the office." She was on her way to the garage.

"His assist.... Mom, where you going?"

"Not far. I'll be right back."

◘

Jeremy was back in his room IM'ing on Facebook when he heard his Mother return. He stood up, went down the hall and stepped into The Duck Room. The television had *Say Yes to the Dress!* on. It was the first time in years he'd seen anything on that TV accept the news or a football game.

"Come in," she said. She had a huge glass with ice filled halfway up with a butterscotch-colored liquid. Upon dispatching her husband, Mary Ann wanted bourbon. Lots of it. She imagined herself standing by a French door in a full slip, sipping finely distilled small batch liquid gold and waiting for her lover, Paul Newman, to arrive.

"What are you doing, Mom? Is Dad coming back?"

"I doubt that, Paul....I...I mean Jeremy," she said as she began opening newspapers and spreading them on the floor. She walked to the wall, grabbed two canvas-backs off the top shelf and set them down on the paper.

"Mom, are you okay?" Jeremy said. His voice was high pitched, a sudden regression to his 'tweens.

She sat down between the two brightly painted ducks and twisted one toward the right, grabbing something off the recliner.

"Sure I am, son. This is just what adults do. Everything will be fine. Funny how I like this show best when the big girls get a pretty dress," she said as she glanced up at the television. "They're so big and so white, the men probably can't wait to turn them into kitchen appliances. Front-loading."

She began laughing so hard at her own joke tears plopped on the newsprint.

Down on the paper, two of Jair's ducks lay on their sides. She picked up the exceptional example from the late 1890s, a Maryland mallard, and turned it over and over in her hands. Its head was still shiny with its original paint, a fact, she remembered, that had tripled the price.

She set it back on the newspaper again and turned it on its side. Jeremy watched her clutch the duck's body as she brought out the little saw Jair used on the gutters, grabbed beneath its little head and began to saw, over and over.

"Mom!" Jeremy gasped.

"This is going to take me awhile, Son," she said as she dug the blade in at an angle. She shifted her legs into a more comfortable position.

"Mom…." Jeremy pleaded.

"Go to bed, Son," she said. "I'll see you tomorrow."

He left her that way, head bent low, wood dust flying. She wouldn't stop until sometime after 2 a.m., when all 87 duck heads, long necks still attached, had dropped to the floor and a huge pile of little beaks sat beside her.

◪

The light failed and Jay had not left the couch. He sat in the half-dark and listened to Dashaun trying to clean the kid up in the bathroom. The kid triggered waves of wild furious hurt in Jay. He right where I was, Jay thought, as he fought off the visions of his own Hell's beginning. This little kid. This one stupid little kid pushed him back down the stairs into the old despair.

Jay took a long pull off a bottle. The more he thought about his childhood, the angrier he got.

He remembered how he and Dashaun had raised themselves. So had their friend Reggie. The three boys grew up together chasing girls, fighting and sleeping on park benches when they were afraid to go home.

Jay didn't like the apartment because, without a Father, he was his Moms' chief babysitter and bottle washer, as if he had birthed his two sisters and wild little brother hisself. He would boil macaroni and mix in ketchup for his brother and sisters before going into the streets. He was 8 or 9.

Dashaun's house was kind of the same except his Moms loved to date hustlers. He hated the men but it meant new clothes and hot food once in awhile. He'd come home from being in the streets with Reggie, aka Ragz and Jay and find Moms and the boyfriend of the month naked on top the bedspread, sleeping off an afternoon of black rock and fucking.

Ragz had it the worst. He had a Father-figure in his house, his Moms' punk ass, drug dealing boyfriend

Craig. He was a Crip. He hated Ragz and Ragz hated him. The last night that Jay and Dashaun saw Reggie, he was talking about Craig and what he was going to do to him. That was more than 15 years ago, Jay thought. Had that much time passed? Jay and Dashaun were parents now, several times over.

Jay heard a door slam and looked up. Dashaun had cleaned up the kid and set him in a chair across from Jay.

"You know your ass is as good as dead, right?" Jay stared at the kid like a wolf ten seconds from culling a herd.

"Yeah," the kid said, looking down.

"Look at me!" Jay yelled. The kid's head snapped up off his chest. "Something so truly wrong with you dumb young motherfuckers. Y'all think this a game? You run in shooting and never kill the nigga you need to hit."

Jay's eyes filled. Dashaun hadn't seen him this upset in years. He took a step towards Jay and put himself between his partner and the kid.

Jay wasn't done. "What the fuck! You think the world owes you?"

"You do," the kid said.

"Oh ho! It speaks!" Jay yelled to Dashaun. He looked back at the kid: "Who the fuck you think you're talkin' to?"

The kid looked down quickly. His eyes went flat and he was back inside himself.

■

"You fucking kill me, man," Dashaun cut in. "You ain't mad at this kid. This kid no different than our situation. He no different than we were. We both wish all that shit didn't happen when we was kids, but it did, Bro. It did. We didn't have a chance back then, and Reggie didn't even get a chance to grow up."

He walked to Jay and sat down next to him on the couch.

"Remember, man? You, Reggie and me? All the time. You remember?" Jay said.

"I remember," Dashaun smiled.

"Yeah." Jay paused for a moment to stare at the kid, then he locked eyes with Dashaun. "Reggie always said he wasn't going to die young and poor. So he planned a robbery. We laughed at him, 'member, laughed in his face? Then he pulled a little revolver from his pocket and waved it around. We still didn't believe it. Then he tell us about his Moms' Crip boyfriend touching his sister. His eyes filled up when he told us. He told us he had to do it. Little boy, crying and waving a fucking gun. Man, we could not talk his ass outta that shit, didn't even believe him. How long since we lose Reggie?"

Jay took a long pull on the bottle.

"16 years," said Dashaun. He kept the names of the dead, birth date and death date, in his head. He never forgot and he was never wrong.

The kid stirred and asked, "so, what happened to Ragz?"

"RAGZ? Who told you my homeboy's name?"

Jay exploded. "WHO? You can't know that name! He been gone 16 years! You coming too close for comfort, lil' nigga. Who you parents? Who you banging with? Some motherfucker in the sett? I'll kill them all. Bet I fucking know them all," Jay said.

"My Moms name is Cherry," the kid answered.

"Cherry?" Jay looked at Dashaun. "We know a Cherry but it's been years. Who is your Father?"

"I never met my Father. He died 'fore I was born."

"That's why your little ass in this situation now. Nobody taught you shit," Jay said to the kid.

"How old you now?" Dashaun asked.

"16. Just turned."

The kid's eyes filled as he looked at Jay and Dashaun on the couch. Jay and Dashaun looked back at the kid. No one moved.

This clueless, bloody lil' nigga was Reggie's son.

◼

A week after Jair's hasty departure, Mary Ann was in the doctor's office. She'd spent a sleepless week, unable to eat from the acid in the back of her throat. She'd hit rock bottom on a Starbuck's scone and here she was, waiting in a reception area. Again.

She sent a group text to friends and family that

said: "Jair has hair but no family. We are divorcing." She finished it off with an emoticon smiley face. Aghast, her friends received a strange answer to their intense queries: "Oh, who gives a fuck." Jeremy received one text from his Father that said, "We'll talk soon."

Mary Ann wasn't talking. Whenever she let her guard down, she felt rage nibbling at the edge of her being. She'd spent at least a half-decade not being cuddled or stroked or fucked and she was furious. She'd believed that if a woman made enough sandwiches and picked up enough dry cleaning, she'd be loved. She'd believed that being married meant you'd have sex; your man would hit your button and you'd shout "Going up!" as you came. She couldn't remember the last time her husband and one of her orgasms had been on the same block.

I can't believe that fat fucker got someone to fuck him first, she thought as the receptionist called her name.

"You need Prilosec," her Doctor told her within seconds of hearing her distress.

"What? That stuff that makes your titties sore?" she cried.

"What are you talking about, Mary Ann?" Her Doctor said with wrinkled forehead. "You have acid reflux. And if you mean Propecia, that's for thinning hair."

Prilosec, Propecia, Whatever. Fuck you old white

guy, she thought.

"And Mary Ann," her Doctor said. "What's with the language? I've known you a long time and have never known you to swear."

"Well Doc, my husband is fucking the shit out of his young assistant. Should I be singing *You Are My Sunshine*?" He blanched and stepped back.

"I…I am so sorry, Mary Ann," her Doctor said.

"Nobody taught me words for this," she said. "No one taught me nice words for disrespect, betrayal and abandonment. No one taught me nice words for GIVING UP EVERY DREAM YOU EVER HAD FOR A FAT LAZY FUCK WHO LOVES WOODEN DUCKS."

"Mary Ann," he said in a soft, fatherly tone. "I think we should do something about that anger. And the birds have nothing to…"

She jumped off the examination table. Her gown was untied and flapping, adding to her look of threatening waterfowl. She stepped in front of her Doctor.

Eyes shining, she looked into his face and said, "Fuck you, Fucker. I haven't even begun being mad. And I've just begun to swear."

She headed out, stopped at the receptionist's counter to pay her bill; rage flaring again as she realized Prilosec did not require a prescription.

What's wrong with popping a Tums, fucker, she thought as she left the doctor's office, $275.00 poorer.

◼

Jay set his tiny son on the floor and walked to the window. He looked back at the blanket on the floor. He was always startled by how little Zachy was. He looked back out of the window.

The bipolar nature of his life twisted Jay's heart. He'd leave a meeting with his homies and come back to pull a Fischer Price Chatter Phone around and around his living room floor. His kids' Mom didn't like what he did for a living, but she sure loved the money he brought home. If he didn't deliver, he heard from her first.

"Fuck," he sighed aloud into the window. Tension built inside him, day in and day out, and he knew he'd have to make a big move soon. But which way. In the streets, he knew exactly where the money was, whom it was connected to, where it was moving and how to get it. In the seen world, he did not have a clue. Raising kids and gang banging was some kind of crazy cocktail. The center would not hold.

Fuck, fuck, he thought to himself. He'd been looking out this same window the day he saw a kid running down the street firing a Glock every which way. It had been difficult to guess what exactly the kid was trying to hit.

"Dumb fucker," Jay muttered into the glass. "Never learned to shoot, scared out his mind, running after some nigga he could never hit in a million years."

These kids, these kids.

He remembered how he and his homie played

Manhunt on the roof of his building. He smiled for a second. Then he thought about Tony. He was 11 years old when he tried to jump between the corner apartment complex and a brownstone and fell.

He'd sent Homeboy Benz to Chicago to check out a business expansion. Benz couldn't wait for the rest of the team and they'd found his body, cut into parts like a fucking grocery store chicken, in an abandoned building on the Southside. He was 17.

He thought about Big Chris. They'd been sitting in the car, high out their minds, plotting the end of some punk ass nigga. They were happy and yelling when a shot was fired into the back of Chris's head. Fooling around in the backseat, Chris's brother was so loaded that when his gun first went off, he laughed.

The pictures in his head were coming faster. He remembered the night that the sett went together to the club. Dead Eye's girl had run to the car to charge her phone. One of Dead Eye's rivals emptied a clip into her face. Her brains were blown across the inside of his windshield and within days, Dead Eye would stick a .45 cap in his own mouth.

Thoughts of Roger, aka The Rabbit, hurt the most. He was the stick-up king and he decided to slow his life down. He was sitting in the park with his 6-year-old son when a guy he'd shot two years before walked up, raised his gun, and blew Rabbit's face off. His little boy held him, covered in hardening blood and brains, until the cops came.

And of course there was Ragz. He had just disappeared. No body, no casket, no tears. Now his raggedy ass son appears. This wound had stayed open, Jay realized. Reggie had been a part of them. They were three and then he was just gone. They had never talked to Cherry because her people came and took her away. Now they knew why: Lil Ragz had been on the way and his dad was MIA.

What do you do with all that death when you were so young? How the fuck do you get out of this shit? Jay asked himself. He didn't know. But he had to get out or he'd die. Or his kids' Mom would die. Or worse. When he thought of his children, his brain clamped down instinctively on scenes of violence. He could not bear it.

I over E, Jay thought. I over E. Every homie knew those two letters meant "intellect over emotion." He'd figure the way out just as he had figured out how to survive and thrive with what he'd been given, or not been given, as it were.

He was a Blood. He had a code drilled into him through ritual and force. The sett came first and if anyone hurt the sett, Jay himself led the retaliation. They beat you; you shot them. If they killed your homie, you killed two of theirs. And if you ran out of the right people to kill, you attacked Dads, Nephews, Uncles, Moms, Sons and Daughters. They weren't off limits either.

He and his leaders told the living the dead were special. Their names were painted on the neighborhood walls and their glorious deeds remembered week after week, month after month, year after year. It was like being promised 100 Virgins but only coming up with slippery pools of black blood and brains, slack mouths, blank eyes, and pain beyond human understanding. He had watched both kids and men try to make sense of the killing and go mad.

Jay looked back at the floor where his son sat. The boy had a Barbie doll head in his mouth. Where Barbie's body went, well, it was anyone's guess. Hell, maybe Dashaun was doing something with it. Jay laughed out loud.

He turned away from his son and pulled out his wallet. He opened it and saw the card. He'd written HAIR across it. Underneath was the name Mary Ann Carlyle and a number.

Fuck it, he thought. It can't get worse.

He picked up his phone and tapped out her numbers.

◼

Mary Ann sat in her divorce lawyer's reception area picking at some calloused skin on the inside of her thumb. She had intended to play Jewel Crush, but the finger caught her attention first.

Her lawyer heard about the duck episode after Jair's lawyer complained about the cell phone numbers. Mary Ann had drilled deep into Jair's emails and gotten his assistant's name, address, and most importantly, her digits. She'd gotten crisp one dollar bills from the bank and written the girl's name and phone number on each one. Then, Mary Ann drove about town buying Tic Tacs, Peanut M&Ms, bottled water and US magazines until all the bills were in play. In those first heady days after Jair's departure, the duck beheadings were simply not enough.

Within the week, an enraged Jair called his lawyer. Seems along with the number there were offers of "French Love" and "Back Door Ecstasy" set Carilee's phone into explosive spasms. Jair's lawyer called Mary Ann's lawyer who called Mary Ann and requested a meeting.

"He's ready to see you now," the receptionist said.

Mary Ann looked up, stood and followed her glumly down the hall.

"Hello, Mary Ann!" her big white and pink lawyer boomed. Mary Ann felt ice crunch in her chest as she moved toward a chair. What was it with me and the pink men, she thought as she sat. This one was a translucent, light, almost ethereal pink, not unlike the canopy on her girlhood bed. Could that be the connection? She was drawn to the last place she had felt safe.

"Hello, Jonathan," she said.

"Hello, dear. You are looking well."

"Yeah?" she said.

"I asked you in…" He paused, looked around the room searching for words before settling on "I got a disturbing phone call."

"I'll bet," she said.

"Did you do this thing with the cell phone numbers?" he asked, smiling.

"Yes."

"Can I ask why?" he said gently.

"I'm pissed," she shrugged.

"Oh course you are," Jonathan's florid soft face bore down on her with kindness. "The end of a marriage is a horrible thing."

"I should have kicked his fat entitled ass out 5 years ago!" she exploded. "What do you want me to do when a fat duck-loving fuck fucks it all up!"

"Mary Ann!" her lawyer admonished. "How are we going to make it through arbitration if you can't hold your temper just TALKING about your husband? You know we are going to be in a room talking to him soon." His face went high pink, the only indication he was having a feeling.

"I know," she said. "I know." Her head bent, she began picking at her thumb again.

"I'm going to need you to tell me all the things you've done. The ducks. The cell phone numbers, everything. Put it in one document. Send it to me. I cannot represent you if I don't know what you've been doing."

Mary Ann dug her fingernail into the side of her thumb and her eyes turned liquid as the sting registered in her brain.

"So you want a list of the bad things I've done? How about this? How about I list all the bad things I

HAVEN'T done. I haven't fucked my assistant. How about that list?"

She stood up, looked down at the big pink face and wet open mouth and knew he was working for the enemy.

"Mary Ann. Please sit back down. We can get this all worked out," he said.

"Worked out? You want me to sit and make you a list of all the bad things I've done? Who the fuck are you? Santa? I'll tell you what I've done: I paid $24,000 for a head of hair that another woman will run her fingers through. I have paid the tuition for my son's school without the help of his Father. I haven't had sex in years. Now you, taking my money and talking to me like I'm twelve years old. FUCK YOU, DAD."

Her exit was a blur and she remembered thinking, How many men will I tell off before this is all said and done? She didn't know but it was starting to feel good. It was starting to feel like she deserved it after all the years of isolation and the birth of feeling, killed over and over, by a needy man. She'd even had a fit a few weeks ago looking at a pair of sized 48 cargo shorts at Orvis. She was in the mall and had entered out of habit, looking for cheap weekend clothes for Jair. Then, she remembered she was getting divorced, realized she was clutching a pair of giant shorts and all hell broke loose in her head.

As she burst through the front door of her former lawyer's building, she took out her phone and Googled

DIVORCE LAWYERS, NYC. Skimming the list of Rosen, Rosenberg, Rosenthal, she landed on Rosenthalerheim, Rachel. BINGO! She thought. There's my killer bitch.

She hit the screen again and the phone started ringing downtown in the tiny office of Rachel Rosenthalerheim.

◘

"I told you ten minutes ago—no onions in egg salad!" Rachel yelled as she raised the phone to her mouth.

"Ah…." Mary Ann's voice was tiny on the end of the line. "Ah…I'm looking for a lawyer named Rosenthalerheim."

"That's me," Rachel said. "I'm Rachel Rosenthalerheim. Can I help you?"

"I'm divorcing my husband and just fired my lawyer. I need a new one," Mary Ann said.

"Why did you fire your lawyer?" Rachel asked.

Mary Ann began hissing air into the phone, blasting out words: "He's fat and he's pink and he treats me like a child, just like my husband did."

"That'll do it," Rachel said.

"My husband is fucking his assistant. We've been married 18 years now. One child. A son. He's pink too. Not my son. My husband. Can you help me?"

Rachel smiled on the other end of the phone. She'd never heard a woman say she was leaving her husband because he was pink. The admission in-trigued her.

"Your husband is pink too?" Rachel asked. "Yup. Pink. Bill Clinton pink. In big khaki cargo shorts. He keeps his phone in his fat thigh pocket. With Velcro. I hate him."

Rachel smiled again. This client would be tons of fun. This client openly hated her ex and that meant a lot more money to a divorce lawyer. It often meant re-ally good stories later. Rachel was a warrior and battle was battle.

"Okay," Rachel said. "Let's get you away from that pink fellow and find you a darker model."

The women laughed, made an appointment and hung up.

◻

Mary Ann found the tiny "Rachel Rosenthalerhe-im, Attorney" sign and rang the bell. She heard the buzz, pushed and was soon in a dark tenement hall, filled with the smell of cabbage. Mail was sliding out of the bottom of the boxes and onto the tiny- bath-room-tiled entryway floor. A man with the beard of a jihadist pushed past her with a collapsible bike. Mary Ann's immediate thought was to run and then she thought, it's just cabbage and Al Qaeda. No husbands here. She continued down the hall to Rachel's office, apartment #1D, and knocked.

"Hey, hey, hey!" Rachel said as she pulled the door open for Mary Ann.

Mary Ann didn't even see the tiny woman in front of her and looked straight over her head at a room full of furniture piled with books, some stacked, though most looked as if they had been thrown. Pictures of Rachel with various smiling brown and black men sitting in exotic locales rested on desks and tables. Legal pads, pages bent back, covered the arms of an overstuffed green sofa. What a horrific color, Mary Ann thought as the cabbage smell hit her dead on.

"Woof," she gasped involuntarily as a dark form below her caught her eye.

"Woof? I'm Rachel Rosenthalerheim. You must be Mary Ann."

Mary Ann's eyes looked at the form in front of her and saw hair. She had chosen some sort of talking fiber art to legally represent her in divorce.

"My hair," she smiled, stepping back. "I have lots of it. I wear it up in court."

Mary Ann continued to stare. Rachel Rosenthalerheim had shiny black curls that hit her perfectly round jutting butt and jumped around as she talked and walked. It was appalling and Mary Ann sensed that men probably found it sexy as hell.

"My husband is bald," Mary Ann blurted.

"Well, you told me he was pink so I'm not surprised. But I have seen some bald men who weren't pink. Come in."

Mary Ann followed the cascading curls several steps in where her foot hit a section of the *New York Post* left open on the floor. As her legs began to slide apart and she twirled into a chair.

Rachel followed and Mary Ann got a good long look at her. She was probably just less than 5' and had the butt of a basketball, almost perfectly round and quite high up on her back. That was the only part of her body that didn't move. Her hair, at least 3 feet long, covered her back and sides with the shiniest, tightest black curls Mary Ann had ever seen. Her sleeveless top revealed lots of upper-arm jiggle. Her breasts were a heaving shelf that Mary Ann wanted to put cans of tomato sauce and low-sodium beef broth on. She knew this tiny, hairy bosomy woman would terrify her husband in way she never could.

"So," Rachel Rosenthalerheim said. "Tell me what's going on."

As Mary Ann told her story, she felt half her life detach and float off like George Clooney over the Ganges. Her eyes stung and tears started. Rachel knew the pain was horrible because the crying had no sound.

"I am so sorry, Mary Ann," Rachel said. "Your situation is, I am sorry to say, all too common. We will get you through this. I promise."

Mary Ann sat in her chair, head bent, hair covering her face. She couldn't stop the tears and had no other thought but to stop them. She knew she was blowing snot all over her hand. Rachel's voice came from miles off but thankfully arrived.

She sniffed, flipped the wet strings of hair out of her mouth, stared at Rachel with shining eyes and said quietly, "I hate that fat fucker."

"I know you do. That's why you're here," Rachel said handing her a box of tissues.

"I wrecked his ducks," Mary Ann said. "I was just...I was just so mad."

"...and you couldn't wreck him, right? See. You're a lot more together than you think you are." Rachel smiled. "But I don't think hurting animals is going to get us any sympathy in court..."

"Oh, they're not animals. They're wood. You know, decoys."

"No, I don't know," Rachel Rosenthalerheim replied. "Your husband collected duck images?"

"No. Decoys. You hunt with them. You float them off into the water and other ducks come to visit the fake ones and then you blow them all...OH!" Mary Ann cried. "It's so sad!"

"I thought your husband was a large pink man from Westchester. They are hunting up there now too?" Rachel asked.

"No. Jair never hunted. He collected duck decoys with his Dad."

"Oh, so your husband's father hunted."

"No, he pretty much sat in a nut-brown leather club chair for 30 years."

"Nut-brown?"

"That's how he and Jair described it. Then they'd giggle."

"I see. But no one actually used the decoys to hunt, ever?"

"Well, Jair and his Dad didn't, but maybe someone did."

"So, these are another man's fake ducks?"

Mary Ann exploded with laughter and tears started again.

"I knew I could make you laugh. After all, I am the great Rachel Rosenthalerheim." She smiled. "If the name alone doesn't get you…"

Mary Ann looked at Rachel and smiled again, much wider. For the first time since she had seen Jair's strange girlie body language while on the phone with Carilee, her entire life felt like her against the world. Here was the first person that might have her back, even if she did have to pay a lot of money for it.

"I did bad shit to those ducks."

"Oh, come on. Like what can you do to a piece of wood?"

"I beheaded them."

Rachel threw back her head and emitted a loud, wet, gurgling smoker's laugh.

"You did? When? With what? Oh God I hope it was with a Westchester hedge trimmer!"

"The night he left. I sat down with the hacksaw Jair used on the gutters and took off their heads…and the necks...."

Rachel Rosenthalerheim again threw that mass of hair back and roared, "Funny, funny, funny!"

"He didn't think so when he found out."

"So this is the 'hair versus duck' arbitration," Rachel said smiling.

"I did some other shit too," Mary Ann said, staring down at her hands, still glistening from her earlier crying jag.

"Like what?" Rachel asked.

"I wrote his girlfriend's personal information on some bills and spent them."

"Personal information?"

"Cell phone number. For a good time, call... you know."

"Oh boy. Well, you didn't saw her head off, at least. But that's pretty disruptive, not to say putting the woman at risk for some really wacky phone calls."

Mary Ann looked back up from her hands, eyes filling yet again. "But I wanted to do her in. Oh, not me personally! I want someone else to do it! Someone in France! I don't know what I'm saying. In the digital age, this was as close as I could get her to the guillotine."

"You know you have to stop that. You cannot go after the mistress."

"I know. I know!" Mary Ann wailed. "I hate her too! Who would fuck that fat fuck!"

"That's not the point, Mary Ann. And you used to,

so don't go acting above such a man. The point is this husband of yours."

"I know. I know!" Mary Ann wailed again. "But I couldn't help it!"

"It's hard not to want to hurt the mistress. But she's not our concern. If she is sad enough to latch on to a man who has to trick a woman into buying him hair..."

"I know. I KNOW!" Mary Ann wailed again. "Have you done anything else, Mary Ann?"

She looked back down at her hands and whispered, "Yes."

"What?"

"Online dating," she whispered.

"What? Inline Skating?"

"Online dating. Dating websites," she said louder.

"What? Like Match.com?" Rachel asked loudly. "What kind of trouble could you get into there?"

"Oh, not Match.com. I created profiles on Prison-Friends.com, BlackKnight, and some stuff I found on Craigslist. Just a few."

"What did the profiles say?" Rachel asked. "Oh...." Mary Ann was now mumbling into her sleeve. "The usual...loves anal sex...nickname is "the human ATM" "...loves to pamper her man with Astroglide ...""

"Anal sex?" Rachel howled.

"Yes," Mary Ann whispered into her hand. "Apparently, the one entry caused BlackKnight.com to crash for an hour because they had so many hits on Carilee's profile."

Rachel smiled. She was so moved by this pained pale woman at her table, acting out and failing miserably to inflict any real pain on her tormentors.

"How many sites, Mary Ann?"

Mary Ann shook her head and was silent. She heard Rachel sighing as she raised her head to confess: "Couple. Oh twenty or thirty maybe. J Date too."

"Compulsive," Rachel said.

"Obsessive even," Mary Ann agreed. They laughed again.

This tiny woman who seemed to be made of black curly hair, flashing black eyes and gigantic butt made Mary Ann laugh more in 20 minutes than anyone she'd known in the last two decades.

Maybe it *is* hair, she thought.

PART II

Mary Ann never answered blocked numbers. Until the troubles, as she had come to call the skirmishes with Jair and Carilee. Before, it had always meant something weird was trying to get into her phone. A credit card company. Friends of friends asking for help or advice. Obamacare kids pitching socialism. Now she loved "unknown" filling her screen: It was always them.

Voice recognition was instant but still the two loved to cloak their phone numbers for the next crank call to Mary Ann. Much of the vitriol swirled around the final night when Mary Ann had kicked Jair out, the evening she was unable to stop calling him fat.

Upon reflection, she understood "fat" did not adequately describe the disappointment of her marriage and began adding words to a list she kept in her head. Thinking about the list sometimes kept her from crying in public spaces or shouting at strangers.

Jair had lost a few pounds in his new situation, and Carilee and he wanted to make sure Mary Ann knew.

Her favorite blocked call had gone like this:

Xylophone music fills the air.
DOO DOO! DOOODLE DOODLE DOO! DOO DOO!

"Unknown Caller" fills the screen.

Mary Ann: Hallo?

Other person: <heavy breathing>

Mary Ann: Hallo?

Other person: <heavy breathing continues>

Mary Ann: HALLO?

Other person: That's right, we're doing planks! Click.

She smiled just thinking of a world where a toned core equaled a loving spouse. Again, her phone started emitting that lovely xylophone music, a choice made to annoy her son. The screen said "unknown" and she felt her mouth fill with saliva anticipating a new exchange of fire.

"Hallo?"

She sucked in air about to yell "stubby bald fuck" when she heard, "M…M…Mary Ann?… Mary Ann Carlyle?"

She sucked in air. Who was this? Thank goodness she hadn't shouted names. Divorce had a feral quality to it, and she needed to be careful in the non-divorcing world. She realized, sadly, she was starting to have some fun with the whole thing.

"Yes? This is she?"

"This is Jay…This is Jason. I picked you up on the road when you was running… you was running from the Mexican church van?"

She froze. The black kid? In that car that smelled like skunk? Oh yeah, and his friend, the chinky-eyed "white bitch" yeller. She'd handed him her card because it's what you did. Great, she thought. He'd actually used it. What now?

"How are you," Jason said. "I wanted to make sure you got home."

"I did," Mary Ann said. "I did make it home. It was a bad day though, and I remember your kindness."

"No problem. How's your husband's hair growing out?"

"Ah...I told you about that, did I? I'm sorry; I was so out of it that day. Ah...I don't know, really. I don't see him much anymore."

"You told us about it....me and Dashaun. Your husband was having problems. With his hair. You had an accident...."

Jay was searching for common ground, something he rarely had to do with women. Looking at him was usually enough for most females.

If Mary Ann could name this feeling—it was somewhere between shame and idiocy—perhaps shidiocy—she would have screamed it out loud. Instead, her eyes burned and grew teary and she felt the familiar burning inside. She became hot and felt menopause nibbling at her edges. And all of this was over hair problems—a man's hair problems.

In a world of melting glaciers, starved children and secret prison cells, her ridiculous life embarrassed her.

She had managed to hit every mark her parents and society had ever set for her, and all she had to show for it was a surly, hurt teenaged son and a Camry with her husband's mistress's molecules still swirling inside.

"It's stupid," she gasped. "We're divorcing. It's not his hair," and once she said it, she started blubbering. These were no quiet tears sliding down her face as they did that day at Rachel Rosenthalerheim's cabbage-scented apartment. This was a loud, gasping, heaving cry. This was a sound you heard at Sea World.

"I'm so...so...SORRY," she sobbed, mouth in a huge O. "I just..."

"It's okay, Mary Ann. It's okay. It's gonna be okay... Really." Jay flexed his hands, looking at the dark purple-black scars that ran across his knuckles as he talked. "Really, it is. It will all work out."

She was crying and heaving for air on the phone so hard, Jay thought she was beginning to sound like the little pile of clothes he had left wailing in the kitchen with Dashaun. That bullshit had started over an iPod, this one over hair. What.The.Fuck, he thought. All he wanted was some light to get in through the garbage he felt piling atop his life. He wanted to have some fun.

She continued to hiccup into the phone and mutter "sorry" from time to time. She couldn't hold onto a conversation now, Jay knew. He understood people in pain. That was his day-to-day business.

"Mary Ann, hang up the phone," Jay said "and cry

for as long as you need to. I'll be here. I'll call you back. And really, don't worry. It's all going to be okay."

As Mary Ann and Jason disconnected, neither person failed to miss the irony—or wonder—of a young battle-scarred Harlem OG consoling a middle-aged white suburban housewife and mother.

◘

She'd been in this community for 15 years playing by the rules and now found herself alone. The only people that cared about her were the people she paid to care about her, like Rachel. Jair, by his very absence, became the thing her son most wanted. His father hadn't noticed him in the same house, but the bond was tighter than Mary Ann imagined. Perhaps they exchanged testosterone handshakes in the air as they passed, she thought.

Maybe the person left behind would always feel the loser and always feel tainted in the eyes of the world. Jair had beaten her to the adulterous punch, a fact that never failed to make her cry. In the end, the love had been gone so long she had thought about nothing but escape for years. Did it matter? Of course not. But lazy Jair arrived at the finish line first. It was inconceivable and her fury kept building.

These moments had no bottom, Mary Ann knew as she heaved. She would cry for hours, stop abruptly, feel fine, and then unexpectedly begin with a new violence she didn't know she had in her. She knew this to be depression: her forbearers would have called it "grief." She had spoken to doctors about it and gotten a prescription for Lexapro. Still the fits came and came and came, a sensation not unlike being thrown to the ground repeatedly by a much larger angrier child.

Triggers were commercials with animals, ads for diamonds, her son's back moving down the hall. She felt a stabbing pain behind her eyes and her stomach and chest had that bad burrito feel. She held this internal state as long as she could but always became exhausted and ceded to the tears. For a woman like Mary Ann, giving in to this fat-fuck-generated pain felt like waking up and finding out she was Kim Kardashian or the Octomom. It was unthinkable, unreal and unfair. Mary Ann was made for better stuff.

She hit bottom when she could no longer breathe. Shortly after the ducks met their end, her doctor kept sending her for CT lung scans fearing a visitation of the tar and nicotine of her youth. He still hadn't ruled out wood dust, and adults were known to develop allergies from seemingly nowhere.

She panted and gasped for air as the doctors waved clean scans in her face. I can't breathe because I'm not alive, Mary Ann kept wanting to yell at them.

Finally, the large black male technician who ran the scanning machine turned to Mary Ann's doctor and said in a voice redolent of The Islands, "She can't breathe because 'er art's broken. Can't you 'ear it, Mon?"

Angels speak from the strangest mouths, Mary Ann thought that day. She dressed, left the clinic, stopped by the side of the car, went into 'recents', created a contact that said "Jason" and began to type away.

◘

Jay fingered through his texts.

U got licks lined up?

He responded with "NO" and quickly got back a text:

B gone. He got kicked out da ride.

Well shit, Jay thought. He'd have to step in and get up some robberies, not his favorite task. The sett was always hungry and demanded dollars for growing children and their restive moms. Parents grew old and needed help. Money had to flow here as it had to flow anywhere. People had families. Responsibilities. Endless need. Jay wanted to burn the whole sorry sad fucked up place down.

He'd been shoving the image of Lil' Ragz'—the bloody bawling bundle of clothes—around in his head since the day the breakdown went bad. He also knew that had Dashaun not been there, he would have shot the kid. The kid was the child of his dead childhood friend, a Blood, a member of the sett. God knows he'd done a lot more over a lot less. Maybe I been at this too long, Jay thought as he touched the next text. It said:

When you gonna sign this fucking lease?

He texted back:

That's it? No hello?

That bitch. Half the scars on his arms were there because of her. Her demands built like tectonic plates crashing inside him and the only relief from his internal pain was to transfer it to the external: Brands, burning blunts, razors and knives helped with all that.

Yet he couldn't ever seem to give her up. Her snatch clutched his cock in a mysterious throbbing way he'd never had with another woman. He didn't even have to move: She sat atop him and pulsated. Together, they had two kids and her daughter from another man in the apartment.

Her gifted twat extended to nothing else. Jay wouldn't call her a chicken head, but she was close. She loved money in the form of new handbags, crop tops, earrings, shoes, pants, skirts, bras, swimsuits and any other girlish shit she could find to buy.

She liked her kids okay but did not spend much time with them. It just took a big chunk out of every day when you were hunting for handbags, crop tops, earrings, shoes, pants, skirts, bras, swimsuits and other girlish shit to buy.

Jay knew in his heart, she would never work a day in her life. He also knew she would abandon and break the hearts of her children while always having enough resources for new handbags, crop tops, earrings, shoes, pants, skirts, bras, swimsuits and other girlish shit, no matter what.

Jason, would you like to meet for coffee? Maybe a mani/pedi? LOL.

Whoa! Mary Ann lives! he thought. He'd reached out to her in a moment of rage over his own balled-up situation and had since become worried about hers. Pathetic, he thought. The Caring Gangsta. He smiled. The Sensitive Nude Caring Gangsta. He smiled wider. God, I'd love to get into that woman, really make her scream.

He hadn't even texted back and already he felt lighter. He'd met people for coffee before but a mani/pedi was a new one. His moms and sisters did their own nails, wads of toilet paper everywhere, mouths running fast and loud. One night Shenay splattered the hall with Mariah Carey aquamarine sparkles and the landlord never did repaint. When they messed up the polish, they'd grimace at the nail like they'd just passed a bball out they ass. He couldn't wait to see a whole room of women doing that shit.

◾

She was wedged between the wall and a tiny table when he walked in. Why had she done this, she wondered, as Jay's eyes swept the room, looking for Mary Ann in a sea of blondes, brunettes and gray-haireds. All these fuckers do look alike, Jay thought as he continued scanning.

Mary Ann saw him but didn't wave him over immediately. What a stupid place to meet. She had typed Starbucks into the phone without thinking. It was convenient and safe. Now she saw this place as he might see it: A room of white people moving through an overly moist environment.

Hissing air forced into milk punctuated a relentless murmur and random pings from laptops and phones. Coffee shops were the new cubicle. People drank skimmed mocha lattes, nibbled scones and waited for rejections online. It had to be rejection, she thought. No one ever seemed to leave.

Jay remembered her blonde hair and her height. Jay was many things: Father, OG, leader, enforcer, lover, brother, son, loyal friend, prisoner, abused child, cutter and killer. But what Jay really was was a leg man.

He had looked at Mary Ann when she unfolded herself from that golf cart of a Camry she drove—out in the middle of nowhere with Mexicans—and something had given in his brain, or his dick, either way. He guessed she'd been at least twenty years older than he was and that excited him even more.

Jay had lost his virginity to an older woman and never ceased to be amazed at their explosive endless capacity for orgasms. Catch 'em at the right age and those gals could pop off all day long. Talk about a Bushmaster, he thought and smiled. Guns and girls, girls and guns. It was the most erotic combination he knew.

Mary Ann stood up, raised an arm and yelled, "Jason! Jason! Over here."

Jay fixed on her position and began moving through the bobbing cups. She noticed he was taller than most people he passed and his hair was slicked back into a short ponytail that rested on his back. The crowded area in front of ORDER HERE seemed to part for him without even looking. He was black and they were all white, sure. But it was also something more. Jay had a power that people felt but couldn't describe: True warriors threw off that kind of heat. It was the feeling of looking at the hind legs of a crouching lion, the flex of talon or the thighs of an NFL defenseman coming off the line. It was power under control, but just barely.

"Hey, Mary Ann," he said as he reached her table. "Hello, Jason. Do I look better without the dust?"

He smiled at her and turned sideways. He began working his body into the chair across from her. At the table next to them, a man with an epic comb-over recoiled.

"Excuse me, Sir," Jay said.

The Comb-Over glared at Jay, snapped his laptop shut, got up and left.

"Fucker," Jay growled.

"No," Mary Ann said. "Do not get angry. Did you see his hair? He's got issues." She smiled at Jay, both of them knowing Jay's blackness had sent the comb-over running.

Jay smiled. "I'm used to it. That's why I don't hang

out much here." He looked around. "At Starbucks."

They both laughed.

Mary Ann said, "I don't think Starbucks has much to do with it. I don't like it either and I have to hang around up here all the time."

"Maybe we can change that," Jay smiled. "You, not the neighborhood. They can rot for all I care. It's hot in here."

"It's all the heat from the coffee-making and milk steaming. And bloviating," Mary Ann couldn't help laugh at her own joke.

"Bloviating?" Jay said.

"You know. Talking out your ass? Lot of that goes on up here. Then they ride the train into Manhattan and do it there."

"I like it. How can I bloviate?" Jay said.

"My soon-to-be-ex can teach you," Mary Ann smiled.

"I'll bet he can," Jay said. "Did he wear khaki shorts and flip flops?"

"Oh God, you know him," Mary Ann laughed. "Take off your jacket. Believe me, you won't be cold in this petri dish."

"You making white people in here? Little carbon? Couple of cells?" Jay laughed as he began to slide off his black leather bomber jacket.

"I think my almost-ex-husband and men that look like him all come out of the same factory in New Jersey," Mary Ann said as she began to really take

Jay in. "I think Governor Christie oversees the molds himself."

Jay looked massive to her, a giant "V" shape that ended at a beaten up studded leather belt.

"Fat boy!" Jay laughed. "We love our Jersey runs. Always buy deep fried hotdogs in that crappy lil' town. Can't remember the name."

She let the words "Jersey runs" play in her head before saying, "exactly." His eyes were black and flashed when amused. He wore ripped jeans and bright yellow loafers, a touch she found quite dashing. Jair never had the balls for yellow.

Jay was really handsome, Mary Ann thought to herself. Thick soft-looking lips. Long straight nose. Deep black eyes that picked up and threw off light. And he was maybe ten years old than her son. But she hadn't noticed that while running from the church van.

Twisting in the tiny hot space, Jay managed to get his jacket off one side of his body and was sliding off the other arm when Mary Ann saw it.

His arms activated some invisible fishhook under her rib cage that began to twist and turn and pull her flesh off her bones from the inside. She wanted to run and she wanted to cry or maybe run crying. She didn't know exactly. She felt wonder, fear, and loss colliding all across this young man's skin.

Jay wore a clean wife-beater that made Mary Ann think of Marlon Brando first and a wife beater second. His shoulders rose up on each side to meet his neck in long trapezoids and twisting sinew. His deltoid muscles were the size of soft balls and the long tail of his large biceps jumped whenever he moved his arm.

As if this overwhelming maleness were not enough, wherever Mary Ann looked she saw skin covered with violence. On one arm, raised white scars left geometric shapes. She also noted a "W", an "R" and a "D" among them. Fine scratch marks hatched up his forearm and three large dark circles stood in a line across his biceps. She took them in and noticed two more, smaller sets of the circular burns on the other arm.

"Orion," Jay said softly.

"What?" she almost yelled.

"The circles. They are from the belt of Orion. In the sky. Stars. I had them branded into my arm."

"Did it hurt?"

"Yes. So do tattoos."

"Why are they there?" she all but cried.

"A symbol," he said, still quiet.

"Of what?"

"My hunting abilities," he said, the edges of his mouth turning up in a Mona Lisa smile.

"Hunting? What do you hunt?"

"People, mostly."

Mary Ann flushed red and her eyes darted downward.

Jay pulled her back.

"I won't hurt you, Mary Ann. That isn't my intention at all. That is so not what I am doing here. My intentions are the opposite."

"I...it's just that…I just don't understand. I don't understand this…what you are….I don't know what I'm doing, obviously….I'm so sorry….." and she trailed off, leaving the female "sorry" to sit on the table, cringing.

"I'm a Blood, Mary Ann. I lead a gang in Harlem."

"You shoot people? From cars? Drive-Ins? Dead people?" she said in a little girl voice.

"I don't. I'm sure some fools do," he said. "And it's drive-bys. Fools in Compton like that shit. That's L.A. We don't do it much here. Maybe a little on the South Side of Chicago….Not here, really." Jay looked into the middle distance, wracking his brain for recent news of drive-by shootings. Colorado stuck in his mind, for some reason.

"So what do you do?" she asked in the same little girl voice.

He smiled. "Mainly, I meet airplanes landing on short runways in the woods."

"That's a weird job."

"Not really," he said. "I unload the plane and distribute the cargo."

"What's the cargo?" she asked, knowing.

"Drugs."

"Oh."

"Mainly ganja, weed. Sometimes other things. Depends on what the market wants."

He smiled again. That white on black was electric,

Mary Ann thought through her anxiety. She felt a change in the air around where they sat, something just below what her senses could process and articulate. He was a dangerous man. He was so handsome, in a beat up, bad boy kinda way, all she could think about was standing-up-sex.

"But you don't kill people," she said, voice lowering.

"Not much any more. I got into management." Again he smiled.

They let the last statement rest between them for a moment.

"I used to smoke a little marijuana in college," Mary Ann said.

Jay was delighted with her use of the word "marijuana." Was anyone this clueless and still living in America? He also found the combination of "older" and "innocent" exciting too.

Great. His boner popped and almost hit the underside of the little table. It's probably gonna get stuck in a wad of gum, he thought. I'm gonna stand up and bring the whole fucking thing with me.

"I don't smoke it myself but if you'd like some...."

"No, no thanks. I'm crazy enough," she said. Then quickly added, "these days."

"Tell me what happened with your husband," he said.

"Not much to tell," she said. "I paid for a hair-transplant and discovered he was banging his assistant. She got the man and the hair. I got the bill."

"How much was it?" Jay asked.

"For the hair? $24,000 and change. Actually, since it went $4,000 over my limit, I also received heavy credit card penalties."

"Hair cost that much?"

"Apparently."

Jay whistled. "That guy is an asshole. Is he fat?"

"How did you KNOW?" Mary Ann squealed.

"Seems to me a guy is obsessed with his hair probably doesn't have a big dick or guns." Jay flexed his. "He's got no counterweight to have him be okay about the hair. Can't get no dick extensions and he don't sound like the athletic type."

"Secrets," Mary Ann said. "He had a lot of secrets. And big titties." She said with clear eyes, to her amazement. Then she giggled.

"Everybody got to have 'em," Jay said. "Secrets, not big titties. But banging your assistant ain't a good one when you married."

"Are you married?" Mary Ann asked.

"Nope," Jay said in a loud grown-up man voice. "Nope, I ain't married. It is not in the plan."

"Why?"

"Mary Ann, are you really asking me that? YOU?"

They both laughed. "Let's discuss putting a ring on it later."

◘

Looking in through the Starbucks window that

day, a Westchester native would have seen something unusual: A white woman beaming into the scar-crossed face of a young handsome black man. Their eyes never left each other and they never seemed to run out of anything to say. She went to the bathroom once in an hour and felt his eyes watch her go and come back. She had a young, beautiful man's attention and her own response shocked her.

I will never live without this again, she thought, walking back to Jay at the table.

She talked to him about everything and he laughed at her attacks against Jair and his mistress. Jay told her some of the things that were true about him and left many out. How could you tell a woman you'd just met that you had stabbed a man 14 times with a screw driver?

The man had been a pedophile and the police would not take action. So Jay did.

He was a Blood, an OG, and people didn't do shit like that in a territory where Jay was King. His codes were strict and always enforced, no matter what. The guy had lived and Jay called him from time to time, just to let him know he was still being watched.

"Mary Ann, what was you doing in the middle of that road?" Jay asked as she slid between the wall and the table.

"Do I have to?" she said with a smile and a sigh. "After all, I wouldn't have known I was a white bitch if I hadn't taken that walk."

Jay laughed. "You *is* a white bitch. No escaping that… and you was walking in the middle of the road."

"I moved over to the side to let you pass."

"You know what I mean."

"I was at the mall," she said.

"What you buy?" he said.

"I'd rather not," she said, looking out the Starbucks window.

"Why you talkin' like you have feathers up yo ass? Why was you at that mall?"

As he repeated the question, Mary Ann could actually feel his power become stronger. He had asked a question and hadn't gotten a straight answer.

"Donuts," she hissed.

"Wha….What the fuck?" he said, throwing his head back to laugh. "You drove all that way for donuts?

It's gotta be thirty, forty miles round trip from where you live."

"So?" she countered.

"So? Why's a grown woman like you driving around with donuts? Why didn't you buy them in town and take them home and eat them?" Jay asked. "You know, open the box, leave it on the kitchen counter, have a donut. Why the mall?"

"They weren't for me," she blurted and looked out the window again.

"Bullshit, Mary Ann. We saw that shit all over your front seat as we drove past. Dashaun was particularly amused."

Exposed, she burst into tears.

"Whoa! Whoa! We talkin' donuts, Mary Ann. WHOA!"

He was up and around the table, smoothing her hair and letting her sob into his torso. It felt hard, she thought as she heaved, and he smelled good. It was a male smell of soap and cigarette smoke, clean and hinting of sin. It's like chipotle, she thought. But he would never want her now, she knew. Not after he figured out what she was doing with the donuts.

Her hair was soft and he watched it flow yellow through his hands. So beautiful. How could anyone not be moved by those two colors together, he thought.

He held her tight to his side, letting her cry and smelling her perfume. It wasn't girly: More the smell of pine or spruce trees. It was almost a male smell and mingled with such a woman, it was a complete turn-on. She held his middle as if she was about to slip beneath black water, never to rise.

"I'm so sorry," she blubbered into his side. "I...can't always control this crying."

"I know. I know," he whispered. "I've heard you on the phone, remember? And it's okay. You just crying that baldy out yo' body."

"Fatty bald fuck," she smiled into his side. Jay remained there until the tears slowed and she was in the hiccupping phase. She hadn't remembered being comforted by a man before. Ever.

Her father had died when she was so young, she

just couldn't get to the memory, if it was there at all. Maybe God had brought this young man to her so she could feel it once before her time was up. She was awash in gratitude, buried her face in his side, inhaled one last time, and released him so he could sit back down.

"Will you promise me something, Mary Ann?" Jay said softly.

"Yes?" she said.

"I mean really swear to it, Mary Ann," he said.

"Yes, of course," she said, eyes still glistening.

"Stop buying donuts and eating them like some fat girl on the run. Eat donuts like a grown-up woman, out in the open, just jam 'em down your face. 'Cuz that some fucked up shit. If you mad, be mad at what you mad at. Don't do this. Don't abuse donuts."

Her mouth went slack and she stared at Jay. He had brought the hammer down on her soft place in the middle of Starbucks. She knew he was right.

Jay had seen straight through her donut drives and jokes about fat people. He knew she was on the run but didn't know from what. He'd spent years on the run too, but the jailer had been different. Now here they were, staring each other down over cakey circles of deep-fried delight.

"You been acting like you got fat girl issues," he said. "Personally, I love issues. I also love fat girls. They fun to ride." He smiled like a devil. "Usually in a woman it means she ain't getting the dick she needs so there's extra enthusiasm."

"Is that the black guy version of 'never fuck a woman crazier than you are?'" she replied.

He laughed. "I love issues. I tease 'em out and lick 'em until they run away."

She felt her throat stinging with the acid of being outed while the "lick em" comment electrified her vagina. One body part burned and the other tingled.

She wanted to touch him, run fingers down his scars, put her hand down against his arm. She was wary of him too, an added bonus when you walked the razor's edge of lust. Sure, he may be a killer and half my age, she thought, but he's a truth-teller. She hadn't met one of those in a long time. She could not believe someone was actually attracted to her, especially when her life was all confusion and pain.

"Why are you doing this?" she asked.

"Doing what?" he said.

"Being so nice to me. Acting like I'm beautiful. Coming all the way out here."

"You are worth the drive," Jay smiled. "You are worth a hundred million mile drives. I knew it when I first saw you in the road and I know it now."

"Impossible to want me," she said.

"But I do," he said.

"Stop."

He was getting nowhere fast and knew she was a shy one, a bolter. Never take a woman before she's ready, Jay thought, and this one would be amazing when it was time. He just had a suspicion. She was so bottled up and bolted down. When she finally came loose, the explosions would be all Baghdad.

"You promised me a mani/pedi," he said. "Pay up."

◼

As they walked past the ORDER HERE counter to leave, Jay raised his hand and put it on the back of her neck, gently guiding her to the door. It was calloused and hot and completely in charge: She would have gone anywhere that hand urged her to go. She closed her eyes, concentrating on the feeling of its heat on her: It was overwhelming. She opened her eyes again, was still walking, and the door to Starbucks swung open.

Jay was still talking to her and smiling. She could see it but heard only the incessant sexual buzzing in her head, a low hum that overwhelmed other sounds. When his voice came in focus, she felt the tugging in her vagina again.

As they left the Starbucks, Mary Ann's pale enthralled face and Jay's gentle hand upon her neck were much remarked upon. Heads bent and fingertips fluttered across cell phones and laptops.

That sweet abandoned woman, Mary Ann Carlyle, was being hijacked by a black man.

◼

As Jay and Mary Ann walked next door into the mani/pedi salon, the brown faces of lovely young women began a sing-song, "hello, hello" to them.

"Mani? Pedi?" the oldest one came up to Mary Ann and asked.

"I just need the pedi. Jay, what would you like?" Mary Ann knew how to be a hostess.

"I want what you having," he said. He looked around fascinated at the bright colors and sparkles, a spy in the secret world of girls.

"Two pedicures it is," Mary Ann said, pulling her signature color "Red Rebellion" off the polish stand. "I'm trusting you to want nude," she said to Jay and immediately flushed.

"No polish. Just clean. Hard to get respect in the 'hood with red toenails," he said. She smiled and thought, how weird I'm about to see this young man's feet. Then she thought, how weird I just thought that. Then her own thinking bored her and she spoke.

"Can we sit in those chairs there?" she asked the older woman who appeared to be in charge.

"Sure. Sure," the older woman said as she began herding Jay and Mary Ann to the recliners perched above swirling waters and tiny footstools. "You, sit."

A beautiful young woman with black hair to her waist sat on the tiny stool before Jay and a flurry of angry Vietnamese filled the air.

"Ong la rat sexy."

"Toi dong y!"

"Toi se lam doi chan cua minh."

With that, the older woman pushed the shoulder of the younger woman and shouted, "Toi la ang chu!" The girl stood up and scuttled off as the older woman muttered "vo on, bitches!" and she sat down in front of him.

"Now, what you want?" she said as she smiled at Jay.   "Just don't paint 'em, Lady," Jay replied. "I beg you."

The room exploded with giggles as the young Vietnamese women stood along the wall, watching the boss and hanging on every word that came out of Jay.

Mary Ann's toenail consultant was not as comely as Jay's, she noticed. She had a wide flat nose sprinkled with pimples. Her hair formed two plumes upward, a pair of chopsticks holding it in place. It was economical, Mary Ann thought, though unattractive.

Mary Ann couldn't bear for Jay to see the dead skin off her feet so she went for the pumice rather than the razor. He went for it all: razor, seaweed wrap, and a 10-minute foot massage. When she heard his deep voice say "toe cuticle," she could not stop laughing. He laughed back.

The room was awash in the happy sounds of foot health. Tubs were filling with water, tiny instruments were being laid out and cotton pads stacked. Jay's toenail consultant picked up one of her metal instruments and shoved her hand in the water, searching for a foot. She got ahold of one and the other came with it. She smacked it down like a fish trying to flop out of a bucket.

"No! No!" she smiled in mock anger, looking at Jay.

He seemed confused as to what she was doing. She began working on his big toe, digging the instrument into the cuticle and pushing it back. Jay's face began to twitch.

"I ….I can't…..ha ha…I can't take this…ha …ha…ha … ha…it tickles," he said as he raised his foot. She held on, rising out of the stool and pulling him back down.

"It tickles. I can't take tickles," he cried.

Mary Ann looked at him. This is where it begins, she thought. This is where it went wrong with Jair, me not calling this shit right here.

"You hunt people but are too ticklish for a pedicure?" she asked.

"Hell, I never had nobody fucking with my foot before," Jay almost yelled, the older Vietnamese woman still holding on. "It tickles when she grinds into it like that."

"It's supposed to," Mary Ann said. "She's cleaning it."

"Should stay dirty," he said just as the faces of the line of young Vietnamese women, standing in line on the far wall, were lit up with red blinking lights.

"Put your feet back in the soaking tub," Mary Ann said as he returned his feet to the hot water. "Let them sit."

"Wha....wha da......wha da fuck…" Jay's attendant said as she wheeled around on her stool to look out the storefront window. Two cops were slamming their doors shut, red light turning without sound.

Officer Ron Heurlin led the way in, his younger partner Jim following. There'd been a report of a black man in the west Westchester Starbucks, and he might have taken a woman hostage.

Standing at the counter, both the older police officer and the younger police officer stood, hitching their pants up and puffing their chests out in anticipation of more human conflict.

"May I speak to the owner or manager of this establishment?" Officer Heurlin asked.

Jay's pedicurist rose, all 4' 9" of her, and walked up to the older officer, a man suffering mightily from waist fat and male-patterned baldness. She got right underneath his chin.

"Me," she said. That was it.

"Okay," he said, sucking in air. "Do you know the man in the chair over there?"

"Yes. He client. We good. You go," she said.

"Now wait a minute, Ma'am," Officer Heurlin said. "We've had multiple reports of a black man taking a woman out of the Starbucks. Is that him?"

"You go," she said again.

"Oh, man…." Jay said as he stared at the police. "The never-ending story," he muttered.

"Jay," Mary Ann said. "I'm so sorry. I'll fix this now.

I know one of them." She stood and walked with wet feet to the counter.

"Officer, no one has kidnapped anyone," Mary Ann said. "I'm perfectly fine as you can see. A friend of mine has come up from the city."

The boss stepped between Mary Ann and the cop and said, "he go."

"I ain't going nowhere until you two tell me what that man is doing over there having a pedicure," Officer Heurlin said.

"Is that against the law?" Mary Ann asked the officer.

"Don't split hairs with me, Lady. What's he in here for?"

"A pedicure," Mary Ann said.

"You go," the boss lady reasserted, still standing underneath them.

"Does he have ID?"

"You are going to card him for a pedicure?" Mary Ann asked, not understanding that racial profiling could and did happen in mani/pedi salons.

Behind them, giggles and splashing sounds became louder. Mary Ann's person had moved over to talk to Jay and the other girls had flocked to him. One had a hold of his hand and was laughing. Another was splashing water onto his foot with a sly smile. A chopstick hit the floor and skittered under a rolling supply cart.

"Go. No trouble," the boss lady said.

"She's right," Mary Ann said, the only white person to defend this room full of brown. "No one has broken the law, Officer. In fact, we're having a wonderful time. I don't see how this is fair, questioning a man when all he wants is healthy feet."

The cop sighed, knew she was fucking with him, and took out his rubber-covered pad of paper. In fact, everything on him was made of rubber except one thing, his gun. Everything else shielded him from his dangerous life, at the moment taking place in a finger and toenail salon. He made a few notes and looked up.

"Nobody ever said anything about fair, Lady. We're leaving. But if we hear you all are causing any more trouble, we're coming back," and with that, Officer Heurlin and his young partner were gone.

As the door closed, the boss lady walked back toward Jay saying, "He go. Good. Me no like him."

◻

Nothing described saying goodbye to a young black man in front of a Starbucks of white faces plastered against steamy glass better than the word "awkward." It was a word she found so over-used, she had banned it from The Duck Room.

Aware of many eyes, the only way she felt she could convey her desire for him was by staring at the scar crossing his lower lip. She could not take in his entire body at once or she might just jump forward like a cat, all four legs wrapped around his torso. The faces behind her would get more than innuendo to spread.

"Mary Ann," Jay said, as he stomped his feet on the concrete, "do you want me to fuck up this "Jair" guy of yours?" He was staring at her intently.

She stood there, watching him move from foot to foot, and somehow she knew this was no idle offer, knew this was some sort of declaration of intention. She also knew he would do it if she so much as formed the word "yes" on her lips or moved her head vertically. The power shift was profound, grotesque, thrilling. So many emotions banged around inside her, the tears just started again.

"Oh, Mary Ann," Jay said. "I didn't mean to..."

Her eyes snapped to his. "No," she said. "You've done nothing wrong. You are so kind to me: It's more than I have a right to expect. I can't remember the last time someone cared about my heart, about my feelings. It is between me and my God when I say 'I do not want him physically harmed or dead.' But I want his life to be as fucked up as I can get it. I want him to feel stupid, lose $24,000, face abandonment. This has been horrific, Jay. This was my work, my life, my family," Mary Ann finished out of breath.

A thin skein of lady-like snot dangled off the side of her nose. Jay wiped it off with the back of his hand, a concerned look breaking apart those lips and scars and dark black eyes.

It had just truly dawned on her, what Jair had

taken, just then. He had destroyed a family, a family she'd given her all to build. The hours of carpool. The PTA, fundraisers, lacrosse practice, games, dances, washing, ironing, kids' parties, doctor's appointments, tutors, home repairs, ladies lunches for worthy causes, cleaning and repairing the house, fundraising committees and bake sales: The stuff mothers build and give without a thanks every day, in and out. Her life's work was over.

Heaving began between tears.

"Okay, okay, Mary Ann." Jay said. My Gawd, he thought. What a beauty. What a broken soul. He stepped forward and took her in his arms.

"ALL them fucking white people got their nose on that glass," Jay whispered into her hair.

Instantly, her emotion turned into hysterical laughter and she began to shake. The vibration did not go unnoticed by Jay's penis. Oh great, he thought. As I stand here hugging her, my cock's going to start doing that "hey lady" thing, digging into her thigh like an insistent finger.

Jay released Mary Ann and stepped back.

"The old 'make him regret-his-mama-ever-looked-at-his-papa" treatment, eh, Mary Ann?" Jay laughed.

She looked past Jay just in time to see a loose dog trot unmolested across a huge intersection, dragging a long broken chain behind.

"A dog would have gotten better treatment from that man, Jay," Mary Ann said, suddenly low-voiced and serious. "His wife was the donkey. And I want to make him regret the day he laid eyes on me. Hell, like you said, I want him to regret the day he was born. And I REALLY want my 24 grand back. If I can't get that, I want the fucking hair."

Jay threw his head back and laughed so hard he felt his pants slip even lower. He'd taken many things in his life, but never a man's hair. He was SO up for this.

"I'm in," Jay said, "as long as you are my partner, day in and day out." He smiled. She smiled back. "And I've never "taken a man's hair" but I'll bone up on my Commanche. They was so gangsta."

"Partner. That's nice, Jay. I don't think I've ever had one of those. Now, please go home or I'll start kissing you and the police will come back. Besides, I have to go get that dog over there."

She walked off toward the dog, knowing Jay was looking at her butt and legs because every black man looks at butts, right?

Jair might notice a vintage canvasback by John McKenney from the 1940's, but the butt of woman? Never. It just didn't occur to him. He was simply too busy blowing through the world, scooping up the next thing he wanted.

He needed to lose some of those things, Mary Ann thought as she got in her car, pulled the dog into the back seat and threw her purse next to her. She grabbed the door handle with a yank and a slam and quietly said through the windshield, "he's gonna lose some of those things now."

She turned the key and drove off to find the dog's family, feeling elated by Jay's attention and the notion she would return a dog, making a happier family whole again.

◼

Jay walked into the house and felt a charge in the air: Rage created interesting wind currents.

Shenay was on him like white on rice, "Now you show up. Where the fuck you been?"

"Damn can I at least get through the door before you start your headache speech?"

"Fuck you. Where was your dumb ass?"

"Come on, Shenay. Do you really have to start this shit and talk like that in front of the kids? I mean damn. It's like your ass never attended a day of school."

"My ass never attended a day of school? *Your ass* never attended a day of school. Oh shit I know you was doing some shit, your ass was doing something you had no business doing. Where the fuck were you? I don't see no money and you know I have been asking you to reup the apartment. You need to take care of the lease. I know I can kiss my dream Audi goodbye. Your ass act like you don't know how to answer your little fancy ass phone whenever I call you. So where were you, besides shooting someone or selling drugs, huh? All you is good for. Oh yeah and I forgot: Sticking your little monster in some big booty bitch."

"What the fuck, are you completely nuts or just bitter? I come home after a business deal to hear this bullshit. I bring Starbucks mocha latti and some raspberry coffee cakes for you and the kids and...."

"Ohhhhhh...latte and raspberry coffee cakes.....," Shenay breathed out with violence. "This nigga didn't just say Starbucks...new this...*Who* are you fucking, because I know your ghetto ass was not at no Starbucks.

"What the fuck do I look like, stupid? Wait until I tell the girls this hot shit. Starbucks." She threw her head back and laughed. "I mean, damn Jay, does every woman have to taste and get a piece of your goodies?"

"Shenay, I swear you are fucking nuts. I bring home coffee and pie and that equals me fucking some bitch."

"You see, Motherfucker, that's exactly what I mean. Your dumb ass don't even know the difference between coffee and latte," again she laughed, picking up the phone.

"Here we go with the bullshit," Jay said. "I'm not gonna just stand here while you talk shit to your stupid friends."

"You damn right," she threw back, dialing. " Hey girl, you not going to believe what this fool tried to pull. Yea girl, he all mad now packing his bag and shit, trying to run out the house because he nasty as hell. I should have got some of that good shit before I made him mad," she laughed again.

"Fuck you, Shenay," Jay said as he began exiting the apartment with a small backpack. "I swear you ain't shit."

Shenay started her edgy cackle and as he left, he heard her shout behind him, "Aw, you know I love you, Baby Daddy!"

◘

Mary Ann made the trip to the city on the train, ending with her head thrown back the whole way she walked through Grand Central Station, marveling at the stars. She noticed handsome men, smelled florals, sweat, hotdog water, popcorn. This building amazed her, made her feel small and huge at the same time.

Thank you, Jackie, she always murmured to herself. Mrs. Onassis had been a driver in the renovation of the building as well as a fashion icon for Mary Ann. Jackie had taught Mary Ann that the sheath covered all. A sheath was good for day or night: all that mattered were accessories and shoes.

Get the right sheath and you got to immerse yourself in a shopathon of accessories. What could be better than that in middle age? For goodness sake, feet didn't get too fat so there were shoes and with handbags, well, no matter! Mary Ann had also begun to love scarves and jewelry, decoration that would have annoyed her in her younger, more active days.

Now that Jay had forbidden Mary Ann to make the donut run, she might swing by Saks on her way home. She'd be saving lots of money on the personal pastries so she would convert it to accessory money and remain financially stable.

As she came through the revolving doors of the train station, a young dark-eyed woman holding a dirty baby stuck a cup under her face and began saying "mah babeee? Mah babeee? "

"Yes, yes," Mary Ann responded, stepping back some. "It IS your baby."

"Mah babee! Mah babee!" The young woman became more insistent.

"She wants money," a swath of gray wool threw over his shoulder as he shot past.

"Don't give it to her!" a flowing red skirt and leather bomber jacket shouted as it whizzed in the other direction.

"She'll starve!" came out of a pile of clothes, sheets of cardboard and a grocery store shopping cart leaned against the side of the building.

Mary Ann and her suburban friends used to laugh and call this "the urban attack." It wasn't so funny, right in the middle of it.

"Mah babeee. Mah babee!" The black eyes grew larger and the baby seemed to become dirtier before Mary Ann's eyes.

"Oh, HERE!" Mary Ann shouted as she reached in to her bag, pulled out a $20, handed it the woman, and took off to the bus that would take her uptown to Rachel Rosenthalerheim's office.

Rachel had summoned her for a meeting that sounded a bit cryptic to Mary Ann. All Rachel said was "Meet me in the lobby of my building and we'll have the results of the 'deep dive.'" Then she'd hung up. Mary Ann could not image what 'deep dive' meant, except something to do with the ducks she had destroyed.

As the bus fired its blast of toxic fumes and began to roll, Mary Ann looked out the window just in time to see her sad beggar woman exiting a bodega, beer and cigarette in hand. The little girl trailed behind her, clutching a Snickers as big as she was.

◾

Mary Ann rang Rachel's bell and was immediately buzzed in. Rachel was in the foyer of the building, waiting.

"I'm sorry I had to call you in with so little notice," Rachel said. As she closed the door behind Mary Ann, she gave it a double yank to make sure it was locked. She said, "too many assholes loose."

Boy, didn't I know it, Mary Ann thought.

"But we have some very good news for your divorce," Rachel said, "and very painful news for you as a wife."

"That's something new, Rachel?" Mary Ann fought self-pity and often lost.

Rachel led Mary Ann off the foyer to a small nook in the lobby with a table with fake flowers and three chairs around it. One chair held a man.

As they moved closer, Mary Ann got a good look at this man. He was so pale and thin; he looked like a sheet of paper. He wore a white short-sleeved shirt and a pair of overly large glasses, like in that movie Argo. (That two hours was about big reading glasses, Jair had said with disgust as they left the theater.) She could not see his face but did notice an open ring binder and piles of bound paper.

"Mary Ann, this is Arch Noblach. Arch, this is Mary Ann," Rachel said.

He rose, confirming Mary Ann's first 'sheet of paper' assessment, and said into his shoulder, "Hello. Nice to meet you."

"My pleasure," Mary Ann said as she took his hand.

He quickly pulled it back and stuck it in his pants pocket.

Staring at the floor, Arch said, "there is so much to do. Shall we get started?"

"You know it, big Arch," Rachel said, giving his shoulder a squeeze. Arch flinched and tried to escape the hand by sliding down into his seat. Rachel just kept talking.

"Arch here is the best in the business. I pulled him off the Vinesteen case to take a look at the husband of yours and his finances. Now there's a divorce.

Multibillionaire husband ran off with a tittie dancer." Rachel smiled to herself, as if wishing all her cases were so much fun. "You see, Arch is a forensic accountant."

"CPA, CFE, and CA as well," Arch clarified.

The lobby went silent. Mary Ann imagined time stopped worldwide when the words "forensic accountant" were spoken. It sounded like death, had to be death, or at least something to do with the end of the world.

"Fo....fo...for.....forensic.....?" Mary Ann could not wrap that word around her mind. She immediately saw blood splatters and bone fragments. She had just had lunch with an Old Gangster but it was this accountant, this sheet of paper, who sent her stomach into the clench of the life-threatened.

"What do you want?!" Mary Ann cried.

Rachel leaned forward. She put her hand on Mary Ann's arm and said, "It's okay, Mary Ann. Arch is on our side. I sent him to find out where Jair hid his money. Forensic accountants trace money pathways and finds hidden income. That's all. "

"Some call me the 'Indiana Jones' of the Excel Sheet," Arch beamed.

"Hid...hidden income?" Mary Ann felt her lower lip quiver and her eyes began to burn.

"Mary Ann," Rachel said with an even low tone, "your husband has packed a Cayman bank account...."

"....with $1,607,632.44 to be exact," the sheet of

paper said, eyeglasses bouncing up and down. Authority filled his voice when he spoke of numbers. "I've seen much larger tax evasion schemes, but this is the New Economy, after all."

"A mill...million...hidden...wha...," Mary Ann did not see stars. She saw her insides, dark and violent, a hatred for Jair moving like a tornado in her belly, up through her chest and then into her head where it exploded out her mouth: "That FAT FUCK squirreled away almost 2 million dollars and tricked me into charging $24,000 for his fucking HAIR?!"

The vase in the center of the table shook when the sound waves from Mary Ann's voice hit it, Arch buried his face back in his shoulder, and Rachel smiled. Nothing ever surprised her when it came to the behavior of men and women. She'd had one divorce that went on an extra year over possession of the husband's mother's wooden salad bowl. It could be that stupid. This divorce, at this high level of financial malfeasance, was not.

Rachel leaned even closer to Mary Ann, "You must be strong here. Your husband has behaved in an unacceptable manner towards you, his family, and perhaps the American government and its people. Let's let Arch explain. He's the best in the business, Mary Ann, and this is a complicated case." She rubbed Mary Ann's forearm like a mother comforting a girl who fell at her dance recital.

Arch's strange baritone voice filled the air. It was so

surprising, Mary Ann jumped.

"Jerald Carlyle has an account with the Grand Crimson Royale Bank of Grand Cayman, a British territory. Three days ago, the balance in that account was $1,607,632.44. Of course, that compounded with interest over the last days has risen."

Arch cleared his throat, closed one folder and opened another. "Jerald Carlyle opened the account in 2011 with a January wire transfer of $200,000 through a complex system of banks in Europe and the Caribbean. He used shell companies. This was a post-FATCA move; quite ballsy actually."

"January 2011? Fat Cat? Who's that? JAIR? What the hell are you talking about?" Mary Ann said, her face again wet with tears and running nose. "He got his bonus then. I thought it was much smaller."

"A year later," Arch continued, "he made another deposit at around the same time in 2012 for $250,000."

"Yes," Mary Ann affirmed. "I remember he said he had a good year that year. But Arch, that bonus was $50,000. I remember. We celebrated with a new duck."

The personal information caused Arch to flush red. He had no idea what couples meant by a 'new duck.'

"In 2012 and 2013, he deposited approximately a half million each January and as far as I can ascertain from the papers Rachel has provided, he has not reported this income to the government of the United States of America. He moved monies through several off-shore banks notorious for looking the other way when it comes to reporting large sums to the American government.

He actually created a somewhat sophisticated system to avoid detection. Of course not clever enough for me." Once again, Arch blushed; paper with strawberry stains.

"Somewhat sophisticated' is not possible for that fuck," Mary Ann hissed. Arch blushed. "Someone helped him."

Arch half-snorted, half-laughed: "It's a 100 billion dollar a year business, off-shore banking. You think these guys are rocket scientists? Hardly," he laughed into his right shoulder. "That I don't know yet—if he had an accomplice. But all will out. Oh yes, when it comes to numbers, all will out," Arch said, the corners of his mouth turned up. "The numbers will not, cannot lie."

"When all our investigations are over, we'll know what we're dealing with," Rachel answered. "Some tax evaders are prosecuted and some fined. It depends on many variables. Had you ever heard of any of this money before, Mary Ann? It's important how you answer this."

"No! Never! Why would I have bought a multi-millionaire $24,000 hair worth of hair if I had known about this? What was the money for?" Mary Ann cried.

"I believe," Rachel said quietly, "he intended to leave the marriage, take the money, the mistress and the hair."

"But that would mean...."

"Yes, Mary Ann," Rachel said, "it would."

The little table became silent as Mary Ann absorbed this new information. Her husband had been planning to leave her for years. He was planning to leave her for years and he wasn't leaving her any money. She and his son would live in a little apartment, alone and diminished. They had done nothing to Jair but love him the best they could.

Rachel and Arch were waiting to see what Mary Ann would do next. What she did surprised them.

"Okay," Mary Ann said, pushing the chair back as she stood. "Our way is clear. Divorce AND prison, if we can swing it."

Rachel smiled, Mary Ann shook both their hands and left the building. Once around the corner, she immediately called Jay.

"He stole over a million! Almost two!" she cried into the phone.

"Whatcho talkin 'bout, Mary Ann?" Jay said. "Slow down, girl. Slow. DOWN."

Mary Ann had stepped into a trash bin nook on the street, yet she could feel the eyes upon her. Even the most focused of New Yorkers couldn't resist a woman yelling "he stole millions!" into a cell phone.

She took in a deep ragged breath and explained, "Jair has hidden almost 2 million dollars in a bank in the Cayman Islands. I have never seen the money, heard of the money, nor did we report it on our taxes."

She gulped in one long sentence.

Jay exhaled. "Mother-goddamned-fucker," he said. "That fat fuck thought he gangsta. I'll call The Banker, Mary Ann."

"Jay," she whispered. "You....you can't give me two million dollars."

"No shit," he laughed, living in an $850.00 a month apartment in one of the most expensive cities in the world. "My people got a banker...bankers. Let me hit up The Banker and I'll holler back. We'll see what old baldy be up to...he a good baldy...he likes having no hair."

"The Banker?" Mary Ann asked.

"Yeah, he be over all the other Bloods bankers," Jay said.

"Blood bankers?" Mary Ann's voice rose.

"You think we got no financial infrastructure? Hell yes we do."

"No...no, I was just shocked to hear that there are 'Bloods bankers', that's all," she said.

"Be nothing but Bloods who happen to work at a bank. We's working everywhere. We is everywhere. We just organize better and take care of our own. Don't worry, I got 'chew on this. I'll hit you back soon."

Jay poked his phone and looked up, relishing a sit down with one of his favorite OGs, a monster of upper management. A gangsta among gangstas, The Banker did more damage in a Saville Row suit than most bangers combined. The Banker didn't end the day washing blood from his dark blue Dickie's work wear: He caused companies to fall and drained the accounts of CEOs and corrupt cops and politicians.

Hell had no fury like The Banker.

◼

Jay was heading to Dashaun's house for some cool-off time.

He punched Dashaun's number, "Yo bro on my way to your house, I'm going to stay a few days. Fucking Shenay, she being an ass again."

"Nigga what you do now," Dashaun said laughing. "I'm glad this shit is funny to you," Jay said. "Just make sure you have a bottle of liquor and not that bull shit you always drink." Dashaun was laughing harder: "I got you, O.G. Homeless."

Jay arrived at Dashaun's house and used his own key to let himself in. The two had each other's back on everything or survival wasn't possible, no less raising a family. Not in this place, not in the 'hood.

"Damn you, what's this 4 months since the last time Shenay kicked your ass?" Dashaun asked.

"Shut the fuck up, I left on my own," Jay said. "Nobody could hear her shit all the time."

For the first time, Jay noticed Ragz sitting on the couch.

He let out a clicking sound and said "Nigga, I can't believe you let that pile come over and watch your TV."

"Not the point. Stop fucking every bitch you see!

"Shenay ain't playing with your ass. Keep it up and we going to watch you on an episode of Snap."

Ragz laughed.

Jay's attention was now directed full on Ragz: "What the fuck your little ugly ass laughing at? You didn't die when I shot you. Just like a damn roach. Motherfuckers never die."

"Yo, Jay, chill with that shit," Dashaun said.

"Naw, fuck that. Why do you have this little shit here with you?" Jay said looking at Ragz with disgust.

"Chill nigga, you in my house. I saying the little nigga good, so he good," Dashaun said calmly.

"Whatever. Where is the liquor? I need a drink," Jay said.

"Yo, Ragz. Take that upstairs. I need to talk to Jay," Dashaun said. Ragz dutifully stood up and walked off with his buzzing, beeping, hand-held gaming device.

He never looked up. "Naw, I'm goin' home," he said as he moved to the door.

"Oh, so you got a home?!" Jay yelled as the front door opened and closed. He turned toward Dashaun.

"So what with you adopting little fucking thieves off the streets now? Giving 'em toys and shit. You give him that game? Somebody blow his head off while he's playing away on the corner."

"Shut the fuck up about Ragz. He the least of it. What you do now?" Dashaun asked.

"Shit, Shenay ass is trippin' this time for real. I can't even be nice without hearing her shit. I brought her some French tasting coffee and some cool ass looking cake donut shit and she got all freaky."

Dashaun let out a rat-a-tat-tat of snorts and laughter.

"What?" He laughed harder. "What the fuck are you talking about? First off, what the hell is 'French-tasting' coffee and what's a 'cake' donut?"

"Fuck yer cake donut. While your ass was off saving little snot nose kids, I found the score of a lifetime," Jay said.

"Fuck out of here, how much is it for?" Dashaun began to jiggle his foot, a sure sign of excitement.

"Unsure right now, but we maybe talking over a quarter mil, bro." Jay smiled as Dashaun's face brightened.

"Say what, my nigga?! 250 is a nice number!"

Jay smiled.

"What's the breakdown? God, we need this. Who do we have to kill?" Dashaun clicked into work mode.

Jay smiled. "This is the killer, we don't have to 86 anyone for the main job."

"What? How that work?"

"Do you remember the white chick, Mary Ann..."

"Wait, what, no Nigga! I knew it was some bullshit...you fucking this white bitch. Is that what all this Starbucks latte shit and watching Friends and Seinfeld is about?"

"What the fuck are you talking about?" Jay countered.

"Nigga don't play dumb. I catch you last night watching that shit. I'm telling your ass now I'm not doing shit with you or her if you fucked her already. You are a fucking mess, I swear."

If a black man could get red with anger, Dashaun would be now, veins popping up and down his neck.

"Bro, shut the fuck up. This is business and I can control myself," Jay defended his record. In fact, it was Jay that had come down like the wrath of God when Dashaun had been outflanked. Why was this nigga questioning his work ethic now?

"Jay, don't fuck with me. I know you and I know your ass is ready to dive face first into those pink lips. You met Nina and the first thing you said was, 'I'm gonna fuck all you friends,'" Dashaun said.

Jay laughed. "I promise I didn't fuck Mary Ann and I'm not thinking about fucking her."

"I'm not kidding, Jay. Do.Not.Fuck.Her. So talk to me, how do you know she is good for this amount of money and what do we have to do to get it?"

"We know she good because she tell us she good. You know what kind of house she lives in and what town. You know where her husband work. We good. But I need you to make a call to The Newark Whale."

"The Whale!!!!" Really? The Whale? Are you sure we need him? Because you know he is going to run us a arm and a leg. And this white bitch, she on you. We get caught holding the expenses, you pay," Dasahun was already adding up the costs in his head.

"Yea, Yea. I know. I know. But he is the only one I know who can get to The Banker, and we'll need to bring him in. He gets the job done, he is clean, quiet and he knows how to handle this large amount of money without anything being traced back to us. Need I say more? The Whale is just a stepping stone to The Banker."

"That means we got to pay them both!"

"Look," Jay said. "Whale only want 15% of the cost of getting The Banker here... Do the math because 15% of $10,000 ain't shit. We hit the assholes who took our weed and brought your son Ragz into my house. We got more than we need to meet this bill."

"Bro, let me ask you something personal," Dashaun said.

"About what?"

"What is it? What do you see in them?"

"Who? What do I see in who?"

"This white girl shit you doing? I mean, I know you Bro. I know how you are with women and how you will never stick to putting your dick into just one. But this feels different this time. I know your ass not fallen for a white girl, Bro."

"You for real with this bull shit?" Jay asked "Mary Ann?" With disgust, Jay said "and what in the fuck would it matter if I was to fall for her? NIGGAS kill me with this bullshit."

"Chill, Bro. You taken this shit all wrong. I'm not judging you at all, I just wanted to know why. To be honest ...partly because I don't understand why. What do you see in them?"

"That's just it, it's not about them. Fuck them. I don't know them. What do I see in her specifically is the question you should be asking. Bro, I know the fear that runs through our people when they see a black man and a white woman in any type of relationship. But guess what? This is not the 60's nor is this shit slavery. So who am I supposed to be still angry at? For real?"

"My thing is you don't believe a huge amount of white people hate our black asses," Dashaun said.

"Really dude? Is that how you truly feel? SHIT, the last time I check we hate black people too. Who is the last white man you killed? Quiet in here, isn't it? Yes, that's what I thought," Jay roared. "The crazy thing about it is we hate ourselves for years. And we didn't learn that shit from white people. We learned by looking into a mirror and deciding to become the men we are."

Dashaun said, "You have a point."

"Think about it, Bro, do you love the Sett? Do you love being a Blood?" Jay asked.

"Yeah, what kind of dumb ass question is that?" Dashaun said. "You know I do. I will die for this and you will too."

"Exactly my point. To love this type of lifestyle is

to except and love all that comes with it. All of it. Last time I checked I don't remember our rivals being white people. He was a brother as Black as night but that never stopped us from putting holes into his body. I mean look at what we are, nigga, we are not human. What world are we living in? We hate it so much we changed our color from black to red and blue and made it the greatest reason to kill a motherfucker? Think of those nights, our mothers cried because they heard another little black boy was gunned down by another little black boy."

"Yeah I know, little boys just like Ragz," Dashaun shot back.

Jay's face went slack as if he was just baited. "Yes, Bro, you're right. Just like Ragz. I am sorry about all of that too, I will work on that. You have my word."

"And you are right about Mary Ann. She is not a bad person. I mean besides the obvious. She will never have a black girl ass."

They both laughed.

"SO we good now? You ready to make this money and live good? "

"Yeah,' Dashaun said. "But just one more thing you have to tell me after you fuck her...."

"What?"

"Let me know if she glows in the dark."

■

"We got to get the 10,000 Gs to get The Banker here... he only fly first class and we have to bring him in from Paris....would the Italians give him a lift? The Banker and the Italians? He wouldn't put up with their guido shit. Collars on their shirts alone would enrage him...he'd twist 'em mid-flight, throw the bodies out and land the plane on his own at Teterboro...." Jay said.

The Banker had a violent reputation, even for a Blood, and had no qualms about red-black stains on a $5,000 suit. He had once strangled his opponent from behind with a limited issue Hermes tie while whispering lines from Lord Byron's *The Destruction of Sennacherib* into the man's ear. Now, it was mostly urban legend as he spent his time in boardrooms, cigar lounges and five star restaurants.

He would go to New York and see these yahoos and have a verbal joust or two with his fat friend in Jersey. The rest of his friends were handsome young men who worked on Wall Street, at banks, hedge funds and or investment houses. Money was his business and his life.

He loved to visit the financial capital of the World where he kept a keen eye on several of these young men's careers. All were Ivy League, impeccably dressed and on their way up. He wasn't a mentor, per se, but an intimate advisor. Mentor suggested a long-term re-lationship and that wasn't The Banker's style. He was grooming them for personal and professional useful-ness and recreational fun.

Whatever was on The Banker's plate, he liked to fly in, do it, and fly out fast.

That's just the kind of man he was.

◼

The Banker sat in a blue-green brocade Louis VXI chair by the fire at the Criterion Club in midtown Manhattan.

His Gieves and Hawkes suit was charcoal gray, light wool with fine blue-green stripes, double-vented. He wore black on black wingtips, a crisp white shirt, ruby cuff links and a thin, deep red tie.

His black bald-head shone with a ferocious reflective firelight and his features had the refined perfection of pure-blooded Ethiopians. His thin black lips were set in an unmoving line and his eyes had a flat, unwavering mystery; black pools where no one got to swim. No one could read The Banker's intentions and that's why he was The Banker. His cheek bones were high and his skin was smooth; he seemed as if he had been exfoliated from head to toe, like a Sony executive back from a corporate retreat. The watch was Hermes. All other needs were met by Prada.

The Banker loved to murmur "It's Prada or it's nada" to sluggish sales clerks and disappear out the store, the big expensive fish that got away.

"Remy XO and a glass of ice water," he said quietly to the waiter as he passed him his empty glass.

"Yes, Sir. Right away."

He picked the *Financial Times* up off his lap. He spread it as a force field in front of him in case any of these old white men wanted to chat him up. He'd been called to the city by The Newark Whale, one of the most vicious of the East Coast OGs—and one of the oldest and fattest—still in the game.

No one understood how he had survived so long in the Game being so fat, but he was a classic case of brains over brawn. The Newark Whale understood financial markets with the same profound insight he understood how to stage an ambush at a four way stop sign.

The Whale was a genius who could have run Wall Street with his friend The Banker, but he applied it to creative ways to kill on the street: he used untraceable ice picks; he'd tie the doorknob shut and burn them out; pitched Molotov cocktails stuffed with nails and broken glass and his favorite, running bleach and ammonia under the door until those lying fuckers breathed themselves dead. All untraceable, all a horrible death.

The Banker wouldn't go just anywhere but there were five or six OGs whose call he answered without reservation. There were just too many punks too twisted up in the wrong shit these days. Everybody wanted easy money without doing their homework and banging intelligently. They were too greedy, too vengeful, too prideful and soon too dead.

But The Banker knew the streets as well as the

conference rooms of UBS and Bank Suisse: He'd started out as a soldier just like everybody else. He'd just happened to get a scholarship from Stanford and studied economics and the markets.

When The Banker graduated, he went home and saw the same sad shit day in and day out. Baby Mamas' whoring for small bills. Hunger. Roaches, rats, drugs, dead kids, high kids, kids shooting at other kids, grown men shooting kids, kids shooting grown men.

He saw it all and moved to Paris. There, a whole new layer of criminal moves was added to his repertoire. He ran with the aristocracy, learning about shell companies, off-shore accounts and hidden tax havens. He learned how the oldest European families looted their way through WWII and kept the spoils. He learned the ins and outs of banking in Switzerland and Austria. These criminals wore British tailoring only. These criminals were smooth and never had to launder a spot of blood off their pricey suits.

In America, he saw piles of money shrinking but never growing. He saw the same mistakes being repeated, creating a rolling insanity across this once great land. He turned down job offers from JP Morgan Chase, Deutsche Bank and Jay-Z.

He began investing for the Bloods and he changed everything. It was the one battlefield the Bloods didn't know how to fight on, and The Banker loved to charge into the fray first, fearlessness wrapped in a Savile Row light wool blend.

The Banker took five of his most trusted OGs—among them The Newark Whale—and set up food banks, micro lending programs, daycare centers, green markets and clinics. No one knew where the money came from and it had to stay that way. Nothing could work unless he stayed below the radar and could move between the 'hood and financial institutions. The only thing that changed between the two worlds was the words and the clothes.

The Banker had blown open new streams of cash. The East Coast was deep into negotiating deals with funeral directors for formaldehyde and veterinarians for horse tranquilizers, all essential elements of new street drugs—PCP and Special K–that white kids loved. The Banker had found the science, production began, and money flowed through the toughest neighborhoods from Boston to the Keys.

The Newark Whale and The Banker had many shared war stories. Their favorite involved two Crips in front of the Gramercy Hotel. The Banker drew instinctively and saved The Newark Whale in an intense firefight that started out of nowhere. After they were stepping over the three dead fools, The Whale and The Banker still didn't know why the three had jumped them. Having countless appointments that day, the two had looked at each other over the pile of dead men, shrugged and went about their business.

The Whale had been humble and refused any special recognition, even the "thank you" dinner at Jean

Georges that The Banker offered. He just went back to Harlem and three years later, the Banker got this text:

Bro, got offshore issues. Can you help?

The Banker texted back:

Require Business Class. Arriving the 30th.

The Whale called The Banker and negotiated a finder's fee of 15%. Then, the Whale called Jay and negotiated a finder's fee with him and told him it was on with The Banker. That was $300,000 in addition to the huge deal of heavy metal from Fort Hood he was hauling up to sell on the streets of Newark: a semi filled with Army issue MP5s, M16s, and even some MK18s, a personal favorite. The street value was insane. Yup, The Whale was having a good day.

Whenever such shipments arrived, the Whale would crowbar one box open, whistle through his teeth, and cry, "let's make war!"

Every branch of the American military had Bloods operating full time, everywhere. They were great soldiers and helped keep heavy firepower on the street. The Whale liked to laugh, "be the Army blasting at the cops" as he fired.

No one understood how such a fat man had survived his full 27 years on the meanest streets in America, before Chicago took that prize from Newark.

"Hell," The Newark Whale loved to laugh, food flying out his mouth as he boomed, "I AM America!"

◘

Nina moved around the apartment excited to meet someone from Paris. She had no idea what he would be like and spent considerable time fantasizing about it as she stuffed celery with peanut butter, set a cheddar cheese ball in the center of a plate and poured Lays into a large bowl her Grandma left her.

Nina's was Dashaun's deeply loving, deeply innocent common-law wife. They had 4 children and she held the group together with a job on the night shift at a nursing home. Sometimes, Dashaun brought home big bonuses and they had a full month or two of toys and new clothes. One payload had been so large, they built a patio, much to the delight of Dashaun's sett. They had even gone to Chinatown and bought him a crimson brocade Chinese robe to wear on his Pat-eee-o.

Few things made Nina more proud than that patio. She'd planted around it, bought outdoor furniture at Costco and began entertaining. Dashaun's sett was only allowed to use Nina's pat-eee-o when she was out of town, but she had set it up for the meeting with The Banker. She knew how important this conversation was to her husband's business.

She was out back arranging paper plates and chairs when the front door banged open like a blast. She looked up to see her husband in full banger uniform, covered with a dark stains on the right leg. Jay's shirt was already in his hand and she could see the red turning black in the balled up fabric.

She walked into the living room, all lilacs and white in her dress, and yelled, "what the fuck?"

"Nina, baby," Dashaun panted. "We put in some work to get The Banker's expenses covered. We be ready to meet with him in a minute."

"Aw right. But D I need you in the kitchen to help with the drinks, so hurry. And don't get any stains I can't get out on the couch. "

"Can do, baby," Dashaun cooed at Nina, whipped around toward Jay and said, "what the hell was that, nigga?"

"My intel was that there was over 50 large in there. Two were the fuckers that came out my house, the ones you chased to the SUV. We handled that."

"Yeah, after having to air out the place," Dashaun said.

The ferocity of the firefight had surprised him. Keysha was everywhere, blasting. He'd brawled his way out and shot twice as much as he needed to.

"How much did you pay Keysha for that?" Dashaun asked.

"Umm, she didn't want any money," Jay said. "But I got our weed back. It has our wrap and had our writing on it. She took some of that."

"Aww come on man. Damn Jay, you need to really stop the dumb shit. You know she is in love with you and you keep sleeping with her and killing with her and one day she is going to snap. She's got gun fever bad, man. She going to kill your dumb ass and your beloved Mary Ann from Gilligan's Island."

Keysha was a Blood who saw both her older brothers die in the wars in Newark. One was shot in the face at point blank range by a short, stocky Crip in a barbershop.

She was trailing behind her other brother Hitz down Lyons Ave, when another Blood walked up and put two bullets in the back of his head over a money dispute Hitz had thought long settled.

Soon after their deaths she joined the gang, tearing her mother's heart. She was sent to Harlem to live with her aunt to stay safe. Within the year, Keysha was banging so hard she was giving her brothers' legacy a run for its money.

She loved her 9mm. Keysha worked as a waitress at a club on the weekends until she had enough money for that gun. She loved it on sight and would never know it had come through her old hometown via Fort Benning and a fat genius of a Blood named The Newark Whale.

When Jay saw her pointing it in a street corner firefight, it was love at first sight for him. Soon, they began killing as a couple. At first thrilling, it became exhausting and a dark sticky horror began to flow through all their interactions.

"I know. I know. But you know she is my heart."

"Her mind is gone."

"She never came back after our first kill together. "

Jay learned two things that day. One was that

Keysha was a hands down killer and two, he didn't think he could have kids with anyone like that. Just now, she'd gone off more than was necessary, much more than was needed. Keysha had crossed the 50-foot line and now had the stare. He had wiped blood off her face on the ride home and she just looked out the windshield, unmoving, unseeing.

She knew why Jay wouldn't be with her and she completely agreed. Despite her reason, it still made her absolutely furious and that frustration often resulted in bodies.

But Keysha knew it was bad enough Jay was fucked in the head, they didn't want two twisted head cases going into a baby.

"Damn that's fucked up," Dashaun said. "Wait, nigga, you two changed in my baby's room before the job. YOU better not have fucked Keysha crazy ass on my baby's bed."

"Come on man, I have more respect than that," Jay said. "I fucked her up against the girl's closet, standing up."

They both smiled.

"Man, I said to her on the way back, 'Keysha, take the money instead. You did the job with me. Stop being so fucking stubborn. She said, 'I said no I don't need your little white collar scheme for money. I am fine without it. I did it for you as I always have."

"She refused any money?" Dashaun asked.

"I told you yes. She do it for the thrillz. And the

smoke. I say 'Keysha, so your ass rather take an unnecessary risk, like that all you know to do with your life.' It's bullshit."

She says to me, 'I really hate you sometimes," she says. "I took a risk with you and for you and now look what I have become… chasing behind you and now you don't even want me. Go live your dream. I'll continue on as I was taught…' I don't even have the words to heal her hurt, bro. She called us a 'beautiful mistake."

"You fucking ghetto Romeo. We ain't got time for this, Mr. Blood, Guts and Sexual Adventure. The Banker will be here soon," Jay said.

"Jesus, what that shit on your pants?" Dashaun asked. Jay was staring at gray and eggshell: He knew damn well what it was.

"Just remember, D. All of this. All of this takes brains." With that, Jay went into the bedroom on the other side of the front door to change. He threw Dashaun a pair of clean pants and a red shirt as he left and he pulled his clean Dickies out of his backpack. He'd even brought his yellow loafers thinking The Banker might get a kick out of them.

◼

Mary Ann drove south into the northern part of the city, a town called Mount Vernon, to meet this banker with Jay and his rude friend. She trusted Jay to keep her safe but had worn her flats in case she needed to run. Since 9/11, most women in the New York area saw high heels for what they were: death traps. Literally, the heel had dominion that day over whether you lived or died. Mary Ann was pretty definite on wanting to live.

She only had to drive around the block twice until she found Dashaun's house and parallel parked across the street. Hey, she thought, now that Jair is gone, I'm even getting good at this. She got out of the car, slammed the door and hit the alarm activator on her keychain.

She looked both ways—though this wasn't midtown, it was a congested area—before crossing the street and starting up the walk. About 5 steps in, she looked up and froze.

Ahead of her was an average-issue apartment building door, dividing two astonishing sights. To the left was a plate glass window with a brightly lit living room spread open to the night. On the right was a brightly lit bedroom spread open to the night. In each room, a man, a man who was black, a man who was black and young, a man who was black and young and very muscular, was in some stage of undress.

Her jaw went slack. She glanced around to see if anyone was watching, looked down, then turned back to the house.

She was in the dark and far enough away from the front door for either man to see her. Dashaun was in the living room to the left, bent over and hopping around on one leg while trying to get the other into his clean pants. His dick seemed to brush the floor with each jump. She gasped. It seemed so long and she saw pink at the tip.

Fairly bright pink too. It hung from a finely defined line of muscle that ran hip to hip, almost like a Greek statue. Jair's pubic area flashed in her mind like PTSD, a white looking pouch stretched downward by unaroused, nubby dick: It was more inverted, jiggly mound than anything. Once Dashaun's pants were on, he turned his back to the window and began to pull the t- shirt over his head. His traps and delts stretched out and every tiny muscle on his back popped and moved. The white of the t-shirt on his latte-colored, heavily roped arms made her—and any other woman who ever saw them—long to be rocked to sleep after a good hard fucking.

He put on the red shirt and flipped his long dreads back and arranged them into a thick ponytail. A cleaner pair of red Chuck Taylor high tops finished the look: He was ready for the banker and moved out of the room.

In the other window to the right of the door, a second personal porno was streaming for Mary Ann. It was Jay, completely naked, and combing his hair back into the low ponytail he favored. She could see his hands working and the flash of his diamond rings. His back arched into a high ass, almost like an adolescent.

His skin was deep black, his scars shining like strips of moonlight across his skin.

His torso came down to the V she had buried her nose in at Starbucks, but now she could see every articulated muscle. He turned and bent and everything was working in his back; there was simply no fat to cover it. He came upright and turned and then she saw it.

Jay's cock was not only long, it was fat, like those pepper grinders they always point at you in restaurants. It moved in the opposite direction he moved, suggesting he was moving fast or it was too heavy to make the turn with him. He bent forward to put his leg in his pants and it too almost brushed the floor. His perfect round high ass was up in the air and she felt a kind of "whoosh" pass through her entire being.

Mary Ann had no words for what she was seeing, feeling. It was if she had to describe the blue of an iceberg, a huge cat contracting in long yellow grass, gold shining up through mud, birth. These male images were hitting her so deep in her gut she had no words. She felt the giant red monkey butt swell and envelope her. She knew she was going down.

Men could look like this? Men weren't nubby and pink? She was shocked, felt strange and somehow humbled. After all, she'd been fighting to save a marriage to old pink tits and look at the riches laid before her. She wasn't sure Jay's penis would fit but she figured if a kid had come out, they should give it a whirl. She could do this and it would change her. Forever.

Mary Ann continued up the path and reached the front porch. She paused and heard a soft voice behind her say, "Did you like what you saw?"

She whirled around to see an exquisitely dressed man, a tad shorter than she, angular features set in a thin- lipped smile.

"I prefer Asian men myself. Not so volatile, much less drama. You can take them anywhere," The Banker said as he rang the bell.

◼

The group retired to the pat-eee-o where The Banker barely took his eyes off Nina for the next two hours.

Even when Jay, Mary Ann and Dashaun explained the story of Jair's hidden millions, all The Banker said was, "Nina, dear, what handbag do you carry with that? My great Aunt Althea, who you resemble by the way, would have worn a Luxe de Ville hinge top bag with a silver handle. Purple, possibly, to match the flowers on the dress. She would clutch the handles just so" and he made a girlish gesture.

Nina blushed, Mary Ann looked at Jay and Jay looked at Dashaun. Dashaun looked back at him like he was the biggest dickhead that had ever lived. His flashing black chinky-eyes said, "we fly this fool in and he talkin' purple with Nina? Who IS this nigga and how dumb are you for flying him here?"

Nina loaded a tray with empty plates and glasses and went into the kitchen for Round II. The Banker's demeanor changed completely.

"She's your wife?" he said, looking at Dashaun. "Yes," Dashaun said.

"Beautiful. Like something from the past. Take good care of her. Or I'll kill you, of course."

Dashaun started wiggling and said, "Now whoa, you're sitting..."

"...on his pat-eee-o," Jay finished. "Banker, what we have is a little under two million in a Cayman account. He is Mary Ann's husband. They are divorcing, obviously, but she came to us for help to recover the funds. We will get a hefty percentage of any recovery effort. Can you help us?"

The Banker put his eyes on Mary Ann, a slight upturn to his mouth to acknowledge their shared vision out front.

"Is this true?"

"So says my attorney and the forensic accountant she hired, Arch...."

"Archibald Noblach!" The Banker finished for her, sitting forward and clapping his hands. For the first time, a full smile split his perfect face.

"Yes," Mary Ann said. "Do you know him?"

"Looks like a sheet of paper?" The Banker asked. "Yes," Mary Ann said. "That's him."

"You are a lucky woman. He is one of the best in the business. He and I have worked together, and in opposition, many times. Is there a reason you do not want to go through official eh…hermm…legal channels?"

"No. Half that fat fuck's money is mine. I used my family's money to raise my son and care for our house. He stashes his and porks the receptionist? I fucking don't think so, Mr. Money," Mary Ann was bright red.

"Mary Ann…Mary Ann…please…his name is 'The Banker'" Jay implored.

The Banker threw his head and laughed. "Yes, I am Mr. Money, aren't I? A character worthy of James Bond. I like your fire, Mary Ann. I would be honored to get you your money. I will require 20% of it."

"Deal," said Mary Ann.

"Mary Ann!" Jay said. "Are you sure you want to do this? You can go through the lawyer and the courts."

"Fuck the courts. I'll be 104 until I see a dime of that money, if EVER, and we both know it. That fat fuck will appeal and delay and jam his fat foot in the door until I am so old I don't care where the money is. NO. I want the money. Had he been fair, I'd want half the money. But hell hath no fury like a woman scorned by a fat bald man."

"That settles it," said The Banker. "I consider this partnership completed then. Mary Ann, your husband is an arrogant, unclever man. He is not my favorite prey: I enjoy a formidable opponent. But you have to take what's available. Arch will up the game, surely, and make this much more enjoyable for me. However, we are not here to have fun. Jerald Carlyle has stolen from the United States Government and he will have to pay. Jay and Dashaun, all I ask of you is that you do exactly as I instruct you without asking questions. Every move we make must be lightening quick. Based on his past behaviors, we can track the money, anticipate its movement and then hit him where he lives. Can you do that?"

"Of course we can," said Dashaun, taking it as an offense that he was a bad soldier.

"Of course we can," agreed Mary Ann, looking at Dashaun, whom she hated to agree with.

"You'll receive texts when it is time for action. My informant inside Jair's organization is a lovely young man. He'll assist on the inside while we make our first moves on the outside. And now, Dashaun, I wish to spend a few minutes with your lovely wife Nina before I depart."

"This way, Mr. Banker," Dashaun said as he led The Banker through the glass doors and inside.

"Jay, you have never spoken to me about what percentage you and Dashaun require," Mary Ann said, eyes cast downward with fear of his financial need and the memory of his huge penis.

"Dashaun and I want 20% as well, plus reimbursement for The Banker's travel expenses."

"So that's about $300,000 something for the two of you. More with interest," said Mary Ann.

"Yes. That means 60% is your share. About

$600,000 and change," Jay said.

"I can live on that. And besides," she said, leaning back and looking at him straight in the eye. "Whoever gets that money first—The Banker, the government, lawyers—hell, I don't care who takes him out."

"Now Mary Ann, that truly is gangsta."

She leaned in to kiss him. God he smelled good, like black fruit punch.

"It's time for me to fuck the Universe back a little, don't you think?" And with that, she smiled, left the backyard and was gone.

A few days after the Patio Summit, Jay got pinged one morning around 8. He opened the message to a photograph of Mary Ann's red lips and the message:

**Lawyers today. I get to see fat Jair.
Wish it were you.**

He smiled. He knew she must feel lonely and nervous, a warrior on her way to a fight. He scrolled through his phone and hit her number.

"Hi big guy," she said.

"You're up early. Have a date with Jair?"

"You jealous?" she giggled.

"You know it. I'm jealous of anyone who gets to be near you. "

Her eyes welled up and she was grateful for telephones.

"That's sweet," she said, voice lowered. "Watch out.

I'm not used to it."

"I know. But it just happens to be true and I wanted you to know it before you sat down across from that fat fool in the lawyer's office. Just remember, chill and we'll get you your money back."

"Oh Jay. I'm just so worried I'll go up over the table and start yanking out his hair plugs…"

God how he loved that image: "Don't do it. We can't buy a car or take vacations with handfuls of white guy hair."

Mary Ann's laugh boomed into the phone and Jay held it a foot from his ear. Was this the mournful woman he'd met at Starbucks? She was coming to life and for him.

That meant horizontal fun in between vertical meetings. Fuck Dashaun because he was gonna fuck Mary Ann and fuck her like she stole something. It would be epic.

"I'll keep that in mind, Jay. And when are we going to have more coffee?"

"I was thinking of something more filling than coffee," he said.

"Oo. I'll let you know how the 'arbitration' goes. I'm just praying I don't smell Jair on top of having to listen to him."

"Sit at the other end of the table, where his smell won't go."

"Good advice. Bye, handsome."

■

They were lounging on the patio that afternoon pounding back 40s.

"I don't want to sell dope anymore," Jay said.

"White chick got you thinking different?"

"It's the losses. When do the losses stop. How do you get out of this?"

"You dawn well know you don't get out of this," Dashaun said. "You're a Blood even when you go into the ground. Death doesn't even let you out of this deal."

"We know this. But do we have to live a certain kind of way? I don't think it's normal to have to carry a gun everywhere I go. It doesn't feel right anymore. Is there an end to gunfire?

"So you're asking if being a Blood can be about something else, something bigger?" Dashaun said.

"Yep. I don't know how and I can't see it yet. But I feel it. There's a life worth living out there somewhere. Be a Blood without blood. Man, I have to do that for my kids."

"'I know, I know, man," Dashaun said. "I worry about mine taking a bullet all the time. I'd kill whoever did it, then put Peggy Sue in my mouth and squeeze. Wouldn't be no reason to be here no more. Dude, your phone's inside and it's ringing off the hook. Next time it rings, I'll grab it."

He disappeared through the sliding glass door and

Jay turned his wolf stare on Ragz. "Hey you little shit, you still alive?"

"I think. You the only one trying to kill me."

"Aw. I wouldn't do that, Lil' Man. You too cute a lost puppy."

"Did you really know my Dad?" "I did."

"What was he like?"

"He was the truth. He was like a brother. He saved my life a couple of times and that's why we saving your ass now."

The scree of the metal door sliding open again stopped their conversation and Dashaun stood between them.

"Bro, that was Keysha's sister."

"What the fuck is she calling me for?"

"Bro, you have to chill before I tell you a thing."

"Tell me what, nigga. Give me my phone. Where is Keysha? And fuck her sister. I don't like nor need to talk to her."

"Bro," Dashaun said, hand on Jay's shoulder. "She is gone."

"What the fuck you mean 'she is gone....'"

"Keysha was shot. She's gone. I'm sorry."

Jay's head went down and quickly snapped back up. His eyes went from white to lines of dark blood zigzagging towards the pupil: "Who did it. We handle them tonight. Load up."

"Bro, it's over and we can't. It was a bad traffic stop. A black female blue and white."

Ragz eyes filled, not knowing Keysha but always feeling his own wounds, and said, "I'm sorry, Jay."

Jay looked down at Ragz and felt a flutter inside that a religious person might identify as grace: "It is nothing to be sorry about little bro. This is the life we choose. Keysha choose it. I need to zone out a bit but before I go. But let me make something clear to you: I don't hate you, I hate myself for not having your spirit. Never allow your wrongs to become your right. *Never.*"

"I promise," Ragz said, awe struck at seeing an OG in such pain.

◼

"What about Jay?" Ragz asked. "He seems so upset."

"He is," Dashaun said. "You know, he cares about you, despite him shooting you."

"I know. We had a talk," Ragz said. "We should call Mary Ann."

"Why would I be calling her for?" Dashaun asked.

"Maybe Mary Ann can talk to Jay before something bad happens," Ragz said. "He likes her, I mean I think he will talk with her and she will make him feel better."

"OK Dr. Fucking Phil, pass me the phone," Dashaun said as they both began to laugh.

He picked up his cell and typed in her number. " Hey, hello can I speak with Mary Ann?" Dashaun said.

"Yes, this is she."

"I know you were not expecting a call from me," Dashaun said. "It's Dashaun and I need your help."

"Sure. Is everything OK?"

"Not really," Dashaun said.

"What happened? Is Jay okay?"

"I need your help reaching out to him. We lost a friend of ours today and Jay has not taken this well. Not at all. I need you to talk to him and bring him back to himself."

"Someone died? Oh my God. Who? Why would he want to speak with me?"

"Because I see the way you two look at each other. He has a thing for you. I know he cares for you. You can comfort him."

"Why have you given me this honor? Don't take offense but I didn't think you liked me. I mean I can't tell if you even talk to white people at all."

Dashaun laughed. "Actually I hate white people. Just kidding. I don't have a problem with you, Mary Ann. To be real with 'cho, I have not seen Jay smile like he is now in years. You take him to a good space. That's where he needs to be. We actually all need each other. One big ass dysfunctional family, a straight soap opera with a talk show on drugs, that's what we are."

"Thank you for letting me spend so much time with you on the pat-eee-ooo. Hanging it, I think you call it. Chillin'." She smiled as she said it. "Believe it or not, being around you all has got me laughing again."

"Alright, alright already, don't start getting all white girl mushy on me now," he laughed again. "Where is the OG housewife who is scalping her little piggy of a husband?"

Mary Ann laughed. "She's right here."

"Are you ready to complete our mission and pull out that last strand of hair?"

"I am riding out with the sett!" Mary Ann shouted.

Dashaun laughed again. "We fucking created a monster! Now we have a gang banging Martha Stewart pulling drive-byes over whose apple pies are better."

"Yes, that's the new me!"

"I'm glad we had this talk and for the record, I do consider you a friend," Dashaun said. "Now please reach out to my brother and get him back on track. We need him for this. Just promise me one thing."

"Yes?," Mary Ann asked.

"You two are really cool together, but don't let me hear about any Bonnie & Clyde adventures, fucking the city up. That's the last thing we needs," Dashaun laughed. "O.G. love birds running around shooting motherfuckers by day and drinking tea and eating cucumber sandwiches when they get home."

"I promise," she said and giggled.

◼

A vicious fluorescent light filled the conference room. On one side of the table, three white men in suits sat in a row, two legal pads with leather sleeves open before them. Jair was in the center. He had more hair than the man on the left and less hair than the man on the right. Their combined weight must have been around 800 pounds. Mary Ann guessed the three had 4,000–8,000 functioning follicles between them.

The other side of the table looked like a cast's break from Sweeney Todd. Mary Ann sat two chairs away from Rachel who was on the far side of Jair. Archie was dead center. The lighting seemed to completely absorb his outline and here he was facing down three giant pink buffaloes. How could this end well?

"Let me begin," Rachel Rosenthalerheim began. "Thank you for having us here in your offices… er….Rosen, Gilder and Stern…we appreciate your hospitality."

"No prob," Rosen said. "Let's get to it."

Rachel's 30 pounds of hair seemed to lift and fall just slightly. "Let's get to it, indeed, Mr. Rosen. Your client abandoned his wife and child. We are looking for one-half of all monies earned and acquired assets from when the two were married, 1998–2015, as well as child support until Jeremy is 18 plus—and I accentuate the plus—four years of college to *any* school of his choice, no matter where the location or cost."

Jair, in a moment of mock surprise, tried to spurt

his coffee out of his mouth. A brown trickle matched his lame response.

 "I don't have that money." He turned toward Mary Ann and half-spat, half-dribbled, "It went to buy you a house and clothes and vacations from your vacation...."

BOOM!

Mary Ann's palm had slammed on the table and she was on all fours, crawling toward him across the conference table.

"You fat philandering fuck....you fat philandering crappy father fat duck fucker...." Mary Ann thundered uncontrollably from some place deep within her being. Vibrations were pulsing out her knees and hands into the table, sending seismic rage toward the suits.

A wall of fluttering pink formed on one side, as Jair and his men began to feel her fury and understand she was moving toward them. Just as Mary Ann reached her hand up to try and grab a hunk of Jair's hair plugs, a piece of paper flew between them.

Jair was gone and a giant pair of glasses said, "NO."

Mary Ann heard the word like a gunshot. She flipped around on her ass and scooted back across the table toward her chair, feeling the first cold creep of shock hit.

Arch Noblach continued his command of the room. "Your client, Mr. Rosen, should not speak directly toward Ms. Rosenthalerheim's client again. What is rightly due our client under the law of the State of

New York has been presented to you and presented clearly. We will retire now to await your counter offer."

With that, the three stood up and left the raking glare of the conference room where three big pink men in suits looked at each other, shrugged, laughed and started high-fiving.

"Freaks!" they boomed.

"Who was that lawyer!" they guffawed.

"Who was that GUY!" they shrieked, thinking of Arch's pale machismo.

And while the penetrating harsh light of the great American conference room ran with childishness, puffed chests, and winning tiger's blood, across the city in a much darker place, great minds conspired to rip the pink from the bones of those fat rosy bulls.

"That went well," Rachel Rosenthalerheim said as Mary Ann drove her and Archie back to the train station.

"I thought it best to stop where we were," Arch reported.

"Good call, Arch," Rachel said as Mary Ann sat next to her, staring at the road ahead through the steering wheel, tears without beginning, end or sound on her face.

Rachel and Arch continued to talk back and forth as if she wasn't there. She made it through two more stoplights before pulling into the parking lot of One World Liquors.

No one would mistake it for a holy spot but it's

where Mary Ann let rip her confession: "I beg both your forgiveness. I don't know what's wrong with me. I used to have control."

"It's called grief, Mary Ann," Rachel Rosenthalerheim said.

"It's beyond that. My rage is so complete that when I saw him, it had nowhere to go. I actually think about murdering him when I'm not thinking of fucking this black guy. That's the only two thoughts I seem to have."

As the words 'fucking this black guy" filled out the interior of the car, a strange smell floated about. Mary Ann now added sound to her tears.

After several moments, Rachel spoke first, "in the city, interracial couples are becoming the norm. Many people on the subway, well, it is impossible to determine the color of their parents by looking at them. I myself have dated many men of color in my life: They are just attracted to me for some reason. Neither Arch nor I are surprised by your words."

"Speak for yourself, Rachel. You have a shelf butt and more black man have dug you than all the trenches in Georgia. As you can see," Arch turned to address the back of Mary Ann's head," I come from people who feel strongly about purity."

"That's what Hitler said," Rachel said. "With that kind of white bullshit...."

"PLEASE. I can't take it," Mary Ann sobbed out. "You don't think it feels weird to me to lust for the one thing my Mamma and Daddy taught me was the lowest form of lust a women could have?"

"You were raised by racists?" Rachel whispered.

"No! They weren't racists!" Mary Ann yelled.

"They weren't racists!" Mary Ann continued yelling. "They were an insurance salesman and a school teacher who told me to never go to the Negro part of town."

"Awk! Did you say 'negro?" Arch yelled from the backseat. "Even I wouldn't do that and I'm Hitler, apparently."

"Look who is falling into an outdated vernacular," Rachel said, staring at Mary Ann.

"Did you say 'vernacular' to me?" Mary Ann asked. "Who DOES THAT in the middle of an argument?"

"A lawyer with Vegas hair and a huge rear end, apparently" Arch said.

"Oh, so now my hair is on trial rather than my sex life," yelled Rachel Rosenthalerheim.

"How did we get on hair?" Mary Ann asked, looking up and sniffing.

"Stupid discussion," Rachel's car voice had returned. "Look, I'm gonna pop in here so I'll have my wine without having to go back out when I get to the city."

"Good idea," Arch agreed. "I'll join you. I love a good blended scotch, a deeply unpopular idea among some of my clients. But there you have it. I'm the man of the people, I guess…"

Mary Ann was dumbfounded. She had just

confessed to her legal team her most hidden, lurid thoughts and they had ended up gleefully shopping for cheap liquor just outside New York City.

The association Mary Ann didn't quite make inside her mind that day was that the 'negro part of town' was now the 'hood, and she was beginning to benefit from its ways.

◼

Jay was shooting down Lex when his phone pinged beside him:

Put eyes on husband.

Army grade. No nanny-cam shit.

He received his first text a few days later from an unknown number. Had to be Paris. It reminded of him of his days with the Italians, sitting in the woods waiting for the Cessnas, digging in to his mosquito bites with a long thumbnail.

Jair was a small plane, he thought with a smirk, but trafficking in white men seemed much more dangerous than weed. No one cared that much about Jay's neighborhood going up in a little more smoke, but a white man, well, they'd care about that. The cops. The papers.

No, they couldn't touch a plug on the head of that hairless cheat but they would get his money and his dignity, just for Mary Ann. And Jay would get those legs wrapped around his neck.

Mary Ann. He imagined her kneeling at his feet,

big eyes looking up into his, an audacious slurping sound filling the room as she ate his cock. He wondered how she'd sound when he hit the back of her throat, so soft yet unyielding. She'd choke and look up at him with sheer wonder at his bigness before diving down for more sucking.

Jay shifted behind the wheel to make room for his expanding dick just as a cab turned in front of him.

Squatting above his seat, Jay laid on the horn and yelled at the other driver, a startled-looking turbaned Hindu, heavily bearded with white hair.

"You want me to send you up to your 100 virgins, you falafel-bobbing motherfucker? Eh?"

After placing an order through The Newark Whale for army-issue wireless surveillance gear, Jay went about wooing Mary Ann. He'd put in work for the sett, put in work for Shenay and then he'd slip North to see the white woman.

He kept Mary Ann up-to-date on plans to snare Jair. He touched her hair a lot; it was just so soft. She traced the scars on his forearm, the self-inflicted ones, and tried to imagine what drove him to sink a razor into his own flesh, over and over again. People, white people, often stopped them and asked her if she was all right.

"Sometimes I feel like no one wants us to be friends, Jay," Mary Ann said after one of these moments.

"Of course they don't. It's subversive."

"What?" she asked.

"Mary Ann, the two of us just walking down the street as friends rocks what people know of the world. It upsets them, white and black. Older and younger. Tough shit, I say. Now somebody gonna tell me who to love on top of all the other shit they tryin' to tell me? Mary Ann, I want to fuck you across the four boroughs, ride you around the triplex, die in your arms. I come up here and we walk around and talk and shit and all I want is to bury my body in yours and forget the shitty life I've had. Wipe out the bloody, lost faces. I want to put my body in yours and see the goddamned sun."

Mary Ann froze. She turned slowly to face Jay and stared at his black eyes. She saw they were open and ready for her to step inside. A gangsta was cracking wide open in front of her.

"Jeremy is at school and won't be home for hours. My house is 10 minutes away," Mary Ann blurted into his face.

And, after unexpressed hours of ruminative lust, Mary Ann committed to the most dangerous act of her life in a second: She would love whom she pleased.

Mary Ann would choose with her vagina and not her head, a path society had lain out long ago and she had been too weak to step off of.

No monkeys with red butts, no deal, she thought, as she raced Jay to the car.

PART III

Mary Ann had often wondered how she'd feel stripping in front of a man besides Jair. In her 5th decade, hairs, dimples and dents had appeared in the oddest places. There was jiggle where there was once bone and a strange ginger-colored hair grew out the side of her neck. Aging well for women took constant vigilance and a good set of tweezers.

She sometimes broke out into inexplicable sweats, even on her shins, and would occasionally look down at her hands and think, who do *those* belong to? None of it even entered her psyche as her nose filled with his smell. His hands were rough and as they traveled down her leg, the care in his touch was an irony that created a jolt in her spine: It felt like a huge cat licking her, leisurely, before it takes her by the neck and shakes.

He ran his hands across her stomach, her most vulnerable older woman spot, saying softly, "this is where the donuts live."

She didn't give a shit as his hand captured the rise between belly button and pubic bone. She didn't even give a shit he said the word "donuts" in bed.

He flipped her on her back like she was a little pancake in a hot pan. He slid his hand beneath her hips, raised her ass in the air, and began massaging it softly in circles. She felt suspended over a huge canyon or a bubbling cauldron: If anyone spoke she'd fall into the abyss. Jay continued softly rubbing her ass before slipping both fingers between the lips of her pussy, pulling it wide open and saying, "look there. Look at how beautiful you are."

She gasped. Jair had never looked at her pussy no less remarked on its beauty. His mouth had never ventured there.

In fact, he liked to call it "lil' snapper" and would say, hot dog tongs in hand while he worked the backyard grill, "I'm afraid of that thing."

His friends in khaki shorts had always laughed.

Jay began to rub the tip of his cock on her exposed wet vagina, pausing to gently brush her clit over and over with the end. Then he spat a mouthful of red wine and saliva, straight down, covering a couple of key holes. She gasped again, and much louder—it was so vulgar and so hot–as he slid his finger around her anus, causing shame and unbearable excitement to join forces and roll around the bed.

"Jay, please…" What the hell was with the spitting, she thought. This is cultural, maybe, she thought as her eyes rolled back in her head with pain and pleasure.

It never dawned on Mary Ellen this was just a good old-fashioned porn move. Her generation had grown up without the sexual mentoring of video. They just had each other's clueless fumbling, and real pleasure was rarely involved.

"Please, what...." He said as he pulled his finger out and put it back atop her clit. Traction was difficult: She was so wet the insides of her legs shone halfway down her thighs. "Please what, Mary Ann..."

"Fuck me," she whispered so softly and with such need, she no longer recognized what she knew to be true about herself.

"With pleasure," he whispered as he slowly began slipping the fat black head of his cock into her.

"Oph..." came out of her mouth, a decidedly un-sexy response.

"It's okay. Okay. I'll put it in slowly... you tell me if it's too much..."

"Okay," she whispered as she looked back at him. "Okay."

He leaned forward, put his mouth behind her ear and began whispering, "you should have been taken like this every day of your grown woman life. You are so beautiful I can't stop thinking about fucking you and now I won't be able to stop fucking you...."

And with each movement, he went deeper, her flesh giving way to his huge black dick as it picked up rhythm.

She flattened herself against the mattress and arched her back up towards his cock, helping, driving, animal- hungry for every move.

Hallelujah, she thought, it fit! That was her last real thought as the world began to disappear and all she felt was Jay's pressure and all she heard was their breathing, their soft 'baby', 'deeper', 'fuck' words that seemed to float over the bed and drop back down for another round.

After hours, she stumbled into the bathroom, not really sure where she was. This must be what being "fucked silly" felt like, she thought as she heard a door slam in the house. Jeremy must be home.

"Jay," she hissed. "Kid is home. Can you go out side door?"

"Sure," he said. "How are you feeling?"

"Better than I've ever felt in my life. Jay?"

"Yes?"

"Do you mind my pubic hair?"

"What kind of a stupid question is that? Of course I don't mind it."

"Jair used to call it Bert"

"Burt? Like Burt Reynolds? He wore a rug. Jair thought your pussy hairs looked like that? Burt's rug?"

"No, like B-E-R-T."

"That motherfucker on Sesame Street with the tuft of black hair on his head?"

"Yes. That Bert. I was wondering if you found anything wrong with my pubic hair? That it was "tuft or tuft-like"–even "fluffy"–or in any way offensive? None of this sounds sexy. I'm sorry. Should I just wax it off?"

"Baby, the last thing your pussy hairs reminds me of is a talking penis on a kid's television show. You looked at Bert? He's a dick tip. Now stay the way you are."

Mary Ann leaned against the door in her bathroom, beaming at Jay as he put his pants back on.

"Jay," she said softly. "Could you say 'bush' instead of 'pussy hairs'?

"Sure," he said, teeth flashing.

◼

Once Mary Ann and Jay had broken the seal on their lust, they couldn't top touching and kissing and fucking. It was all on the down low from her son and all their friends, making it even sweeter. She felt God was repaying all the years of celibacy by creating this perfect young man for her. And he appeared to love every inch.

Jay proved a kind of Dr. Doolittle to her sexual Eliza Higgins, teaching her the cowgirl, reverse cowgirl, jack hammer, and side-scissor. She was penetrated from the front, behind and each side. They took props to bed: pillows to create angles of delight and even a dildo, introducing this suburban wife and mother to double penetration. Jay was an Ass Master and he discovered a love of teaching while he was with Mary Ann.

As she unloaded clean dishes, he came up behind her, sliding his finger up her shorts, playing with her clit until she ceased all action. He began sliding her short little pants down and she released a deep moan atop the clean glasses. Now, with elbows on the counter and torso stretched across the door of the machine,

Mary Ann felt Jay eat Mary Ann her from behind. His tongue was wide and hot and knew just what crook and cranny to linger in to send her to a land where no dishwashers or washing machines existed.

He cupped her breasts as she ironed Jeremy's school shirts and climbed in the tub with her and bathed her like one of his kids, making her squeal and laugh without a thought as to how much water her stomach displaced. She'd dribble bubbles down Jay's white strips of skin, amazed that two people with so many wounds could feel this kind of joy. It was a feeling she believed was gone from her life forever.

Now she understood she never had it in the first place.

◼

"Who ironed your shirt," Kessler jeered. "A cat?"

"No, Kessler," Jeremy sighed. "My Mom."

"She forgot the whole left side, dude," Kessler laughed.

"She's got some new boyfriend. He takes up all her time. I'm pretty happy to get this half of an ironed shirt these days…."

"Boyfriend? Your Dad took off when…?"

"Few months ago," Jeremy said, his voice heavy with the exhaustion of dealing with idiotic parents.

"No grass growing on your hot mom. So who's the new man?" Reichler cut in.

"Black dude. Some guy from Harlem."

"For REAL?" Kessler asked, deeply skeptical.

"Yeah. He works with a group of men she met at the Mall. Mom only said they had something to do with agriculture and aviation. I don't know much more than that."

"Oh man. Harlem! Your mom fucking a black dude is the coolest thing that has EVER happened to you, man. I've never even met anyone from Harlem," Kessler said. "Will you invite me to meet him?"

"I don't know if she'd like that, but yeah, I can try."

"Harlem. Wow. Wonder if he's a gangster like on TV. Omar! Cam'ron! Or maybe more Denzel in Training Day. No matter what, it's awesome," Kessler said as he cleaned up his lunch wrappers, picked up his tray and stood up. And, in that way of all teenagers, he let a cruel bomb drop with ease as he shot "bet he's got a huge 'swipe'" over his shoulder as he walked away.

"'Swipe?' said Reichler.

"That's what he calls his dick. He thinks that's the sound it makes when it touches stuff," Jeremy explained.

"'Swipe," said Reichler with a look of wonder on his face.

"It's just his weird shit man, don't lose your place," Jeremy followed Kessler's path to the trashcan and back to class.

■

"Goddamn this thing is big," Dashaun said as he unpacked the wireless surveillance camera The Newark Whale had run up the East Coast from Fort Benning.

"She-eet," Ragz said, turning it around in his hands. "Guy will see this, D."

"I know, little bro. I know. Doesn't seem like The Newark Whale has it all figured out when he sends something this big on a civilian mission."

Ragz rolled the camera in his hands and read aloud "long range PTZ camera..."

"Now what da fuck we gonna do with dat? Newark Whale must think we peeping the Barclays Center. We just need to see a bedroom, man."

With that, Dashaun picked up his car keys, and he and Ragz set out for Costco in search of more prudent spyware. On the ride over, D told Ragz his favorite joke about the nigga and the Cadillac dealership. Caddy salesman says to the nigga, "you thinking about buying a Cadillac?" Nigga says, "I'm GONNA buy a Cadillac, I'm thinking about pussy."

Ragz didn't get it but Dashaun laughed at his own joke for blocks.

◘

Ready to do some work.

The text was short and sweet from Dashaun to the Whale, who would forward it on to The Banker.

Surveillance had been set up and now they just needed instructions on what they were looking for.

Dashaun and Ragz had chosen an appropriate wireless nanny cam at Costco and Dashaun bought the kid a little game and some new Dickies. Half boy, half man, like all the rest of us, Dashaun thought as they checked out.

Getting into the gated community where Jair and Carilee lived was simple. Dashaun borrowed Johnny Z's locksmith truck and he and Ragz waited on the street outside the entrance. As soon as a resident returned, they followed them through the security gate and straight to the office.

"Looking for a Carlyle," he said, clutching a clipboard he found in the truck.

"Must be Jair and his sweet wife Carilee," a gray haired woman of indeterminate age and unyielding hairdo said.

"Carilee is not the wife, Ma'am," Dashaun said. "That's Mrs. Carlyle a few towns North."

"Oh, oh, how sad," the woman said, grabbing the side of her cardigan. "He's run off with this young woman?"

"Apparently," Dashaun said. "You know what they say about the heart of men..."

"No, no I don't, young man," she answered. "What..."

"Sorry Ma'am. I am really on a tight schedule today. Mr. Carlyle—I work on his other house where his wife lives—asked me to come and work on the lock here. Can you tell me where he is?"

"6B. Is there a problem?"

"No, not at all," Dashaun smiled and the room lit up, Broadway-style. 6B as in bald, he thought.

Feeling a kind of loosening in her stomach, the woman smiled back, pulled a key from the wall and said, "I know you're a locksmith, but this will make it easier."

"Thank you, Ma'am," Dashaun said. "I'll be sure to return it when we leave."

"You're a lovely young man."

"Thank you and you're a lovely lady," he said and was gone.

What had stuck with Dashaun about Jair and Carilee's love nest was the sheer vulgarity of it: Not everyone had Nina's taste and style. This place was all stairways with beveled glass, fake flower arrangements, and everywhere, oversized pieces of furniture bought with an eye toward a much bigger house.

This bitch wants a McMansion, Dashaun thought as he slowly climbed the stairs with Ragz in search of the desk and computer where they would install their electronics. Ragz, behind him, had his finger on the mirror, making the high-pitched squeak of a window-washer across glass.

"Quit that shit. You don't know who's in here. What I got to do with your ass? You leaving behind prints. You gonna die before you get started if you don't start using your head," Dashaun's black eyes bore into the kid.

Ragz fired back with the universal childish look of wounded surprise, "Who me?"

They walked down the hall and turned left into a bedroom. It was bare except for twin beds.

"Fatty ain't in here," Dashaun said.

"Shhh, you don't know who in here," Ragz mocked.

"You little....smsh....it's a good day for a lesson..." Dashaun said in a flat, controlled voice as he picked Ragz up and hung him by the back of the collar from a coat hook on an open closet. "Your sharp-ass nigga bitch tongue can chill here while I do this thing...."

Ragz eyes were huge: No one had ever hung him on a wall before and just gone about their business while he dangled, alone.

He could hear Dashaun moving around in the next room, shifting furniture, the thump, thump, thump of smaller objects hitting the carpet, a loud chuckle and then silence.

Ragz thought about the electronics that might have been had in there—he wanted a Bose like The Banker said he had and loved—and felt more than a pang of resentment at his punishment.

Dashaun was back in the room without the camera, pulling Ragz down off the wall.

"We out," he said as he began walking fast down the hall. The kid knew to follow. He couldn't take another hanging.

Dashaun and Ragz climbed back in the van and

Dashaun peeled off his gloves as he started the engine.

"One more detail," Dashaun said as he reached into a bag and pulled out his laptop. He opened it, grabbed some WiFi and clicked. There was Jair, big router left unencrypted and hanging out for all to see. Just like his butt crack, Dashaun thought.

Using the IP address, within a matter of minutes, Dashaun had burrowed down through Jair's computer. He now had every email ever sent or received.

Jair was as sloppy with his cache cleaning as he was with his marriage. He had never wiped it out and now Dashaun, fierce Newark Blood, warrior among men, wrecker of the peaceful dreams of white people, had the entire history of every website—relative, doctor, accountant, pornographer, priest, colleague, client, corporation and most importantly, bank—Jerald Carlyle had ever visited.

Dashaun smiled, snapped the machine shut and swung by the office. He returned the key to Six Bald and left the old woman with one last electrifying smile.

That smile would, four years later, be the last thing she remembered before slipping into forever after a bout of vicious pneumonia.

◼

"What's with all the ducks?" Dashaun asked Mary Ann when she and Jay were on the pat-eee-oo with him and Nina one afternoon.

Her eyes filled with tears. "He's doing it to another one," she said. "I thought I would be the only one."

Jay and Dashaun shot each other a "what the fuck?" look while Nina leaned forward and patted her arm.

"You will be loved again," Nina said to Mary Ann quietly.

Graceful Nina.

"Oh God, it's not that, Nina!" Mary Ann all but shouted. "Do you know how many ducks I gave him? Was it enough? No! It was never enough! He wanted an older, rarer mallard on each birthday, at every Christmas. He wanted a Holmes for Christ sakes! They are worth six figures at auction! But that's not even it.

"Oh, I'd stand before him, breasts bouncing, and he'd be looking at ducks. He'd pretend to be looking at me, but I could tell.

"Then he wanted other stuff too. A Lexus. A Lexus SUV, for one kid! We were the joke of the neighborhood, everyone in their Chevy Suburbans full of kids and here came 'the one embryo Carlyle's' driving down the street. But the one thing I will never ever forgive him for was tricking me into buying him $24,000 bucks of hair for another woman to run her hands through. I will never forgive that fat man for getting laid while I sat thinking about 'the good of my family.' Now he's got her buying him more ducks to replace the ones I whacked. Predatory fucker. Steal a woman's joy and make her pay, in money, in wooden ducks, I don't give a fuck. But P-A-Y."

When Mary Ann finally sat back in her chair, pink-faced and losing steam, Nina, Jay and Dashaun began to roll this duck thing around in their heads.

"What is the duck reference?" Nina asked.

"Oh for fuck sake, it all bores me so," Mary Ann hissed into the Universe.

Jay, ever the diplomat, told Nina he'd tell her about the duckpocalypse later. And that night, on three separate pillows, the idea "white people like ducks" danced through the slowing thoughts of Jay, Nina and Dashaun as they were sucked into dreams full of ponds, lily pads and shotguns.

◼

"Louder!" Jay said.

"Louder than that?" Mary Ann said, popping her head up.

"Louder. Really fill the room with it."

"Okay, if you say so…." Mary Ann's head dropped back down to Jay's cock and began to make the sound of an entire soup kitchen working their spoons on a Bowery winter's eve.

"Suck it like a lollipop…"

"Oh, like those big ones that go round and round?"

"Yes," he said, "those."

"I don't really see the diff…"

"Well there is one," Jay said. "Really get that lollipop juicy."

As Mary Ann's head dropped back down into position she thought, kids talk a different dirty these days, and soon she had a loud sucking and smacking noise going that seemed to please Jay. He moaned and began to sway slightly. She reached around his hard stomach and clutched his high ass cheeks. As she pressed her mouth harder against his cock, she felt she was taking in his essence, breathing in the core of his being, touching the root of Jay or, as Jimi Hendrix would say, digging his Earth.

"Spit!" he yelled

"Spit?" she was back up at waist level again. "I will not. It's disgusting."

"It's not disgusting. It's hot. Spit on my dick and make it really slippery…"

"Spit on my dick," she muttered as she dropped back down and did as she was told. "Spitting on your genitalia seems so disrespectful…"

"Just spit on it! Make it juicy…oh yeah…oh…, " he started to sway again, "now, look up at me…." he said.

She immediately stopped and popped back up, rocking back on her heels.

"How?"

This chick's a fuckin' meerkat, Jay thought, before he said, "No, no not like that, Mary Ann," Jay said. "You are supposed to look up at me as you suck."

"I'll lose my balance…"

"No you won't…"

"Will to…"

"Mary Ann…for me…just keep your eyes on mine….I won't let you fall."

"Okay…I'll try…"

As she began to suck and smack, she looked up at Jay, brown eyes boring into black. And as they locked into a twisted eyebeam that seemed as if it would hold them together forever, Mary Ann felt her left knee, an old field hockey injury, give way and collapse.

She hit the floor in agony, still trying to maintain eye contact and clutching Jay's glistening dick.

◼

"Mary Ann," Rachel Rosenthalheimer's voice boomed from Manhattan one morning, "we have the counter offer from your husband's attorneys'. I need not tell you that it is not good nor is it fair."

"No, it's Jair," Mary Ann said, smiling at her own wordplay. "Mind if I ask you what he offered?"

"One-half the house, about half the child support you asked for until Jeremy turns 18 and nothing more. You keep the Camry, he keeps the Lexus. No mention of additional funds beyond what we can see of his 401K, checking and savings account. Basically, this deal means a man worth 2 million gives his wife of almost two decades about $175,000 after all the closing costs.

"That's about .04 cents for every day of your marriage. Great respect for value of your life, that one."

Mary Ann felt it again: a burning metal pole in her stomach and a wet stinging in her eyes that could not be blinked away without great huge tears flowing down her cheeks.

"I.HATE.HIM.SO.MUCH," Mary Ann said softly, empathically.

"I must admit, I am coming in at a close second these days. He IS an asshole, though no lawyer should ever tell you that about your ex."

A muffled sound rose and a scream of NO NUTS rose from the phone before Rachel came back on and said, "We need a powerful arbitrator because this is going to become ugly, I can just feel it in my bones. Arch agrees. We should have had one at the last meeting. My bad.

"And you being a lioness and all ready to spring off a conference table at a piece of meat. I mean really, don't do that shit again. I'll reiterate our requests of one-half of all assets for the duration of your marriage. We will let them know we are willing to go all the way to court, if need be, because the evidence of abandonment is so compelling. No one cares about this," she said, "except people at the country club."

The final statement—about the country club—was the only information that penetrated Mary Ann. Social pressure. Colleagues. Clients. Country Clubs. Prestige. Pink. Bald. Men. Jair.

"Okay," sighed Mary Ann. "Set up an arbiter."
"Arbitrator."

"Fat fuck."

"You cannot lose your temper. They are baiting you. And I guaran-damn-tee you at the next meeting he asks for sole custody of the kid. Never seen a man in my life who didn't try during a divorce proceeding."

"What?" Mary Ann screeched. "That man didn't know if that kid was alive or dead most days!"

With that, Mary Ann begged off the phone, promised to behave, and fucked the freak out in a way she no longer knew possible. She cried. She yelled. She stomped her feet. Her chaotic thoughts were all Jair: Jair working late and missing Jeremy's game, Jair refusing to lend the car, Jair taking the kid to the batting cages, an outing that ended in a week of silence between Father and Son. Jair Jair Jair was an okay, not-so-okay parent when he wanted to be. And if he was there.

Sole custody?

Fat chance, she thought. This request was a rocket launcher aimed at her head. She remembered the troops she had marshaled behind her and her heart rate began to return to normal. That fat man best watch it; the counterinsurgency had begun.

◼

WE LIVE

...was the text Dashaun sent to The Newark Whale who would send it up the chain of command to The

Banker. In the meantime, Dashaun went about setting up a kind of "pulse center" in a corner of the garage. From there, he and Lil' Ragz could monitor the ex and execute The Banker's instructions.

"It's your first job," Dashaun said to Ragz. "Some peoples commute to Wall Streets, you come to my garage."

They ran all the wires from inside the house through a thin hole they drilled in the particle board. Dashaun's PC was now sitting atop an old ping pong table. He laid out 4 CSM burner phones, all bought in different states in case he had to call The Banker or The Newark Whale fast. The ole' 401K will have kicked in before anyone could trace these phones.

And Dashaun, being Dashaun, taped a Kimber Micro KDP beneath his computer on the underside of the table and a long machete to the table's leg. Headquarters now had a security system to match his reputation. Machete was his street name, after all, and it was a gruesome hit: Your face was torn apart but you didn't die. You lost a finger, but you didn't die. You lost a hand, a foot, a breast, but you didn't die. You didn't die; Machete made sure of it.

Ah man, he thought, finishing the final touches on his home office, those were the days....

◘

He didn't like it. He didn't like it at all.

The Banker had allowed his new designer to talk him into giving up his beloved 19th Century XVI bureau plat for his new desk, a single sheet of graphite marble which was, even he admitted, a more powerful presentation.

He would miss the mahogany with ebony bronze mounts and leather insets; they were in perfect condition and pleased him deeply. He liked to think of all the deals, legitimate and not, signed during the 200 years that desk existed.

"This rock does have a good feeling," he said in impeccable French. "It is as unyielding as I am. Ship the Louis the XVI to my new friend in New York. He'll look magnificent working at it."

"Yes sir. It will cost a great deal to transport it that far. Are you sure you won't like us to find something comparable already in New York?"

He turned to his designer, flashed a huge smile, and said, "oh, he's worth a little transportation cost, mon cherie."

He walked back to his new monolithic desk and picked up a cheap little phone buzzing across his desk.

"Good….my end is in place…within his brokerage house so we are in the computers….yes….we can share feeds….hold on, I'll call you on 5515."

The Banker hung up the burner and handed it to his assistant. She would incinerate it. He pulled another burner off the slab of marble and dialed a number that ended in 2202.

"We have the shell companies all mapped, I believe, and the route is not complex. He only passes through two before he deposits in Switzerland. He moves a tiny portion at that moment and pays taxes on it. From the shell company to Switzerland, it makes one last move to the Cayman Royale. He pays no taxes on that. Seems he's bought land in Roatan. Change to 4949."

The Banker hung up the burner and handed it to his assistant for incineration.

He dialed a number that ended in 1212.

"...must be going to run off with the mistress.....but who runs off to HONDURAS for the love of God...I mean why not San Salvador! Panama! Ecuador!...crappy little countries....he should stay in the Caymans where there is some civilization...a bookstore...Wi-Fi...*cuisine*... It's part of Britain, for god's sake...O Whale...I wish it wasn't some cliché motivation every time, but I guess running off with young pussy is as big a part of the American dream as the wife and kids...the mistress and the Islands...Mon...."

They shared a laugh, an unspoken dislike of Island dudes hanging on the line between them.

"Don't be hating on Honduras. They have those shark whales. Reminds me of me when I was a boy," The Whale's laugh blew up the line. "I'll be in Paris next week, then Lyon."

"My fair city?" The Banker asked in mock surprise.

"You know it. Can't get this fat just livin' in Newark."

Again, the two men laughed hard before each relinquished their phones to the fires on their respective sides of the Atlantic.

◼

A day after the command center had been set up, Dashaun was practicing throwing a basketball into an aluminum trashcan when Ragz called him over.

"Fucker, this isn't a new video game. This is my computer."

"I know, Dashaun. Sorry man," Ragz said. "But look, people are coming into the house."

"What'cho know?" Dashaun said as he moved toward the computer.

"Yeah. Two white people and they both fat. Come look," Ragz said.

Dashaun came up behind Ragz and saw all the potato chip crumbs on his computer screen.

"Move over and let me see. Damn you little shit, you made a mess over here with all of these snacks and shit. Where do you think you at, the movies?"

Two white people, the man in a dark suit and tie and the woman in a flowing dress with rhinestones between and beneath her breasts, came bursting into the bedroom underneath Dashaun's camera.

"Damn they seem drunk," Ragz said.

"Of all the women in the world and with all that money, this damn fool found a chubster..." Dashaun said, shaking his long dreads. "He's got himself a fatty, a moped, a curvy gurl, a woomyn."

"A moped?" Ragz asked.

"Yeah, son," Dashaun said as he put his hand on Ragz shoulder with mock parental authority. "They are lots of fun to ride but you wouldn't want your friends to see you. A mo-ped."

They giggled and looked back at the screen. Now both their subjects were sitting on the bed partially nude.

"Dude," Dashaun said laughing. "You watching this shit here? Who belly is rounder? Hers or his?"

Ragz and Dashaun began laughing. "Looks like we are going to witness a sumo wrestling match tonight."

"Maybe she is pregnant," Ragz said.

Dashaun looked at Ragz, an endless well of disbelief available to how naïve the kid really was.

"Yes, they are both pregnant with wedding cakes."

The garage filled with more laughter.

"Roll 'em in flour and head for the wet spot," Dashaun added. "Oh man," he said, wiping tears from his eyes. "These white people are great. Dude, look at them, they barely can wrap their arms around one another," Dashaun said. "And looks at their cute pink toes! His stomach is swallowing his dick and her stomach is sticking out more than her chest. Have you ever seen seals mating on the TV?"

Ragz said, "What do you mean, like on Natural Beographics?

Dashaun's chest had puffed back up and he had resumed his position of concern next to Ragz' chair. "Yes, this is mating season on the island. Two seals are beginning their ritual and, at any moment, he is going to bite her on the nose to complete their timeless dance."

"Look," Ragz said. "He freaking out. He's coming out of the bathroom and he looks like he's yelling at her."

"Probably wondering where his Viagra went," Dashaun said with a dazzling smile. "Ha!" Dashaun picked up a jar of pills and began shaking them. "And I took the shampoo out and refilled it with some shit Nina put on her legs. I don't know what that goo is but it smelled like sheee-it. Can't be good for the big boy's hairs."

Ragz looked up to him with wide eyes. He wasn't sure kind of goo a woman would put on her legs that smelled like sheee-it, but he was sure it couldn't be anything great for Jair's hairs.

"Look at him run from one side of the room to the other, bouncing and belly flopping around," Dashaun said, unmoved by Jair's distress.

And Carilee? Dashaun had to hand it to her, she did not abandon her flopping lover's flesh, even his dick as it jumped around like a sardine the waves left behind.

◼

"He's prone to cold sores," Dashaun giggled to Ragz the next night when they were watching the action in the walrus cave. "Mary Ann told me when Jay wasn't listening."

"No kissing, Jair! You'll get the pink eye," Ragz yelled for no apparent reason.

Dashaun picked up his phone and sent a text to The Whale:

> **Tell his whole company he got herpes.**
> *What?*
> **Tell The Banker to tell the husband's company he's got herpes**
> *Why?*
> **Tactical.**
> *You kids*, The Whale texted. ***Point taken. Adversary shaken. Consider it done.***

◼

Jerald Carlyle felt great as he pulled his Lexus into his underground parking slot. He'd eaten a beautiful dinner last night, had great sex and a wonderful night's sleep. What could be amiss in the world, he thought? His mind landed on Mary Ann momentarily and the words "scrawny bitch" floated through but he didn't allow himself to dwell on it. Carilee was helping him to not think toxic thoughts.

At the security desk, he smiled as he did every

morning but the security guards did not smile back. They watched him warily as he put his identity card down on the turnstile's glass, eyes following him all the way to the elevators.

A scattered few waiting for a ride up did not notice Jair, a couple took several steps back. When an elevator going to their floors, 35–59 arrived, he noticed they did not step on with him. Odd. It took 4 minutes for these elevators to come back down. Four minutes was an eternity in New York City.

He stepped off the elevator opening his suit jacket. The floor's young receptionist stared at him, looked down at her monitor, then stared back.

Without warning, she then let out a short high scream.

"What are you doing?" Jair said through clenched teeth as he charged her desk.

She leaned back as if the bubonic plague was lolling on her stapler and slowly turned her computer monitor around so Jair could see the screen:

Employee Bulletin:
Jerald Carlyle will be out of the office with a viral strain of herpes. He can be reached at home or on his cellular telephone, 917.626.2153.

Jair let out a scream, with more bass than the receptionist's, put his hand over his mouth and walked with long steps toward the bank of elevators.

◼

As soon as he was in the safety of his Lexus, he punched Carilee's number. She sat in the cubicle outside his office: She'd know what this horrible IT snafu was all about. Those sub-continentals, he thought, remembering the Indian computer experts who tumbled into his office, hair moussed into rhino peaks.

"It's the blue cable," they'd say before one would become agitated and yell, "it's the red cable!" and they'd all start dialing their phones. No one knew where these guys worked in the building: Jair suspected they were in the basement pushing emails into tubes and blowing hard so that they'd reach the desired floor.

"Jerald Carlyle's Office...."

"WHAT.THE.FUCK."

◼

*Carilee always got to work at least ten minutes before Jair: They were still on the down low at work. Of course everyone knew and called them the "Blubber Lovers" behind their backs, while seething inside that these two were getting some and they were not.

"I opened my computer and there it was on the daily Cooler Chat email. I ran to Susan and Joelle's computers and it was there too. Someone has played a trick on you."

"Get it off," Jair screamed. "Get it off!" A colleague passing Jair's SUV glanced in, sure he was fighting off a bee.

"It'll get handled," Carilee said, a pale large Olivia Pope saving her man. As Jair punched off his cell, he thought it must be that asshole Brian Leopold; he wants my job. Or maybe that new guy, the handsome one, the one with the old French desk, Jonathan Bottum; I got the bigger bonus. He prances around and can't keep up with me! But herpes, that was low, lower than these guys. It was that new kid, Winklehaus, that furtive fuck. He's smart. I'll bet he's a hacker. No wife. No kids.

■

Carilee picked up her company directory and quickly punched in the four numbers.

"Vishnu!" she barked into the phone. "There's been a breach!"

"A b..b..breach?!" Vishnu replied. "I see no data leaking...."

"Can you actually see data *leak*, Vishnu? This breach is internal, a breach of both privacy and chain of command. Someone has gotten into the company email and circulated something very unpleasant about Mr. Carlyle. He is a partner, you know. Who is in charge of Cooler Chat?"

"Amar is in charge of sending the Cooler Chat each day," Vishnu said.

"Can I speak to Amar?" Carilee said.

"Amar has not yet come in for the day, Ma'am."

"Oh. Have him call me as soon as he does. I'm at 4649.

"Tell him what it's about."

"Yes, Ma'am."

She dialed Jair's cell. "The old IT guy says one of the young IT guys runs the Cooler Chat and he's not in yet."

"Well, call the old IT guy and tell him to call the young IT guy on his cell and tell him to get his ass in here because Mr. Carlyle wants to see him."

That girl wasn't always the brightest bulb in the lamp, Jair thought, the first cracks beginning, far beneath his consciousness, in his love for Carilee.

◘

Hours later, Amar and Tarik emerged from Jerald Carlyle's closed office door. While no "breach" had been found, the boys were in charge of the Cooler Chat and both swore no one else had access to account. After some time, Jair's superiors came in along with Vishnu.

They had decided to issue an apology, say it was a prank pulled by a kid who got ahold of a password.

Corporate jocularity all around.

"You are worse than your Uncle Tana, the goat fucker," Amar spat at Tarik as they left the conference room.

"For the love of all that is holy, I am from Mumbai. There cannot be goat fuckers in my family. We cannot keep them."

"You made up the name of a guy who doesn't exist! You can't lie to the company!"

"Oh, come on man! You were willing to take a fall because Jerald Carlyle has a cold sore? Who *knows* who would care that much about him. You should be taking me to Taco Dream right now."

"Who the hell is Madmusoodam Chaturvedi? Where'd you even get the name? Who the fuck could pronounce it?"

"Exactly. And we're Indian. He's the guy that wrote the email," Tariq smiled. "I'm betting these guys would rather let the whole thing slide rather than appear stupid trying to say 'Madmusoodam Chaturvedi.' Big pink guys in suits hate to look stupid. They'll pay thieves millions just so they don't have to admit they've been robbed. It's called a 'write off,' and believe me, I'll never let old Madmoo near a computer again."

"Okay, I will take you to Taco Dream now that I see your fiendishly clever thinking…I never thought about an Indian playing the race card…"

"Well, do more than think about it," Tariq smiled. "Play the race card and win, bro."

◼

That night, a huge mound of Jair and Carilee was centered in a California king bed under a quilted bedspread, large purple flowers Jair recognized as lilacs splashed all over it. Carilee had wanted a "female" bedroom; she wanted to create a nest of pillows, dried flowers and floral upholstery. Jair had agreed, conceding his duck room would be his man cave. Carilee, in a nod to Jair's passion, put a decoy and small bunch of dried cattails above the television cabinet. It was here Dashaun nestled the nanny cam. The angle made objects appear larger than they actually were.

"I can't believe those Indian pricks," Jair laughed as he changed the channel.

"Yes. The internet age is swift and uncertain," Carilee said. "In college, I was bent over when a boyfriend took a picture of me. Viral did not begin to describe it. But I got it down and I got him kicked out of school."

Across town, Dashaun and Ragz stared at the computer, looking like they had just smelled limburger cheese.

"Can you imagine what dat looked like?" Dashaun said. "Holland Tunnel is my guess. With thick pink flaps."

"Das the grossest thing you ever said, dude," Ragz objected.

"Someone actually did that to you?" Jair asked Carilee, a sudden swelling of respect for her bravery in the face of great humiliation. "I don't know if I could have taken it."

"Oh, I had the last laugh. Ever hear of the revenge fuck?"

"Well, no, I haven't," Jair stammered.

"My friend Doralece is a good example. She fucked a black man to get back at white men for stealing black men's music."

Dashaun and Ragz looked at each other, confused, then shook their head sideways violently. White people logic. And that back shot of Carilee was not leaving their minds' eyes quickly either.

"Yo yo, this big girl is a pussy terrorist of some kid," Dashaun whispered at Ragz. "She be using it for no good."

Ragz laughed. "They *all* be using it for no good."

"Shut your mouth, kid," Dashaun said. "A woman, a woman like Nina, well it's not 'no good.' It's the best. And it will be the best for you when you grow up and fall in love and have an even lil'er Ragz."

"So, who did you fuck?" Jair leaned forward, kissing Carilee softly on the lips. He reached his meaty hands beneath the covers and began to pleasure this feisty young woman who had saved his career today.

She leaned her head back and let out a low moan and Jair whispered it again, going deeper into the fantasy of Carilee's revenge.

"Who did you revenge fuck you juicy, sweet, cumming woman...."

"Oh....oh.....ahhhhh" she said as her back arched, "....his d-dad........"

◘

When Jair hired Carilee, he saw what most other people saw as well: an almost fat, quiet girl with red hair and a big smile. He had thought, "hmm, a plain Adele" when he'd first seen her. He didn't remember what they had talked about that day in the interview, but she was immediately available and money focused. She was in the right place.

In the first week of work, she'd utterly changed his life. She synced his calendar with the corporation's, cleaned up all his contacts and *added in street addresses,* an antiquated touch that charmed Jair. She had memos, corporate profiles and spread sheets sorted and ready for him to study in multi-colored files marked Monday, Tuesday, Wednesday, Thursday, and Weekend. She even initiated the firm's first dipping-of-the toes into social media, an event that made this closed world extremely fearful. Carilee assuaged their fears and had a dignified Facebook page up and running in a couple days. The page said nothing, had pictures of pink men, and 2,000 likes she bought with Jair's corporate card. They loved it.

"I know, money never sleeps" she had smiled, when she showed him his new system of 24/7 organization.

Within weeks, colleagues noticed a more together

Jair. He started to make more money for the firm and Carilee became integral to every move he made.

"Why you pushing that crap company on old man Richardson," she'd ask and Jair would look in her color coded files and realize she was right.

"What should I push?" he'd ask, a puppy on Wall Street.

She hadn't begun this job wanting to turn her boss into her slave, but since the situation presented itself, Carilee went with it: "Twitter."

"That's your suggestion for old man Richardson? *Twitter?*"

"You asked," and she'd be gone.

He would pass on her words as his and did nothing but make money for his clients. His bosses noticed and his bonuses grew.

Carilee, for her part, hadn't considered herself to have a predatory inch in her body. In college, she'd lost her figure, slowly, to unbaked cookie dough, pizza, French bread and Nutella. She'd lost her heart to Howard Rijinsy, an intense young man from upstate who was studying accounting.

She and Howard had a happy junior and senior year until he dumped her at a graduation party underwritten by a Wall Street recruiting firm. He wanted to be free to pursue his dreams, wherever they led him. She thought he was reaching as to how excited the world was for his talents and agreed a little too quickly for his comfort about splitting up. They parted friends, whatever that meant. I mean, really, she thought. If you dump me, you expect a card on your birthday? The friends thing merely soothed wounded pride. Meaningless, thought the pragmatic Carilee.

Her parents were surprised she felt so little grief for Howard and were even more surprised she wanted to move to New York City. Immediately. She remembered her mother had once said, "Carilee, you aren't the type to wander far. You'll end up back in this town, married to your high school sweetheart. I mean, as a baby, you wouldn't even crawl off the blanket..."

Two weeks after graduation, Carilee took all her savings, gifts and clothes and got on an Amtrak headed North. She found roommates in a weekly free newspaper and got the first job she interviewed for. She couldn't believe how easy it had been and started spreading the news. She *was* gonna be a part of it, New York. Her life would not be small after all.

As Jair's dependence grew, her strange attraction to him began and grew with it.

She started to wear low-cut tops to work and joined a gym. She experimented with make-up. New York was a fine place to learn how to be a girl and she took advantage of the clothing shops, nail salons and goo stores. He noticed. They started eating lunch together at small restaurants several blocks off the beaten path. They soon graduated to hotel rooms above her gym, where their sex life began one noon.

As she watched Jair's hunks of money come in,

that green worm began turning in her chest as she lay awake at night thinking about how to get some of the great things that kind of money could buy. Her large lover was a golden goose.

Thus began Carilee's hard fought campaign to woo Jair out of his home and tie her destiny to his. She didn't have any great gift: she just showered him with the things withheld her. She told him he was handsome, left him sticky notes that said "kill 'em" before big meetings, and brought his favorite dulce de leche cronut from the place she passed on her way from the bus. In short, she paid him attention. Lots of it.

Now she could almost see that house in Roatan, a Honduran heaven where her cruise ship had docked that time.

◘

Strolling with Jay on the Battery one day—they had a lunch date in the city—Mary Ann got a call from Rachel.

"Honey, it gets no better than this. Our arbitrator is Dawn Long. She's known among divorce attorneys as the 'Pocket Hercules' and has unraveled some of the messiest, angriest, bloodiest couplings of the last decade.

"She may be a little person but she's got huge cojones and deep down inside, I know she dislikes men. Not that she prefers women; She just finds men lame.

She's consistently sided with Moms on custody issues and is beyond reproach professionally. Simply can't be bought.

"She is really gonna hate that bag of dicks your husband is dragging around."

"Bag of dicks?" Mary Ann said. The visual was immediate, squirmy, chaotic and appalling.

"I knew Dawn in law school. Even then she more than compensated for her size with her legal mind. Why she chose to arbitrate divorce, I'm not sure. I always took her for a prosecutor."

"Why do you keep bringing up her size?"

"She's a little person."

"She's a little person? What does that mean? You're a little person, Rachel."

"No I'm not. I'm quite normal. Dawn is a little under 4'. She suffers disproportionate dwarfism: shorter limbs, larger head. They call her 'the pocket Hercules'. Behind her back, of course."

So, I have two little people and a sheet of paper for a legal team, Mary Ann thought.

"When will I meet her?" Mary Ann asked.

"Not until the next arbitration meeting, scheduled a couple weeks from today."

"What do we do at that meeting?"

"Rebut their rebuttal. Counter their counter. Chat about adultery. You know, the usual."

Mary Ann smiled as she stood next to Jay, river wind sending her hair everywhere as she stared across the harbor at the Statue of Liberty and talked to her lawyer. Jay leaned in and put his arms around Mary Ann, keeping her warmer while they stopped for the call. Founding fuckers, she thought, I want love and liberty too.

"We keep our same strategy," Rachel continued. "Well-educated woman who gave up a potential career to be a wife and mother. On every not-for-profit board in town. Civic minded. Exemplary behavior for almost two decades and the husband takes a lover who he also supervises at work. The liaison is discovered and you must therefore end the marriage as an example to your son."

"When do we talk about the money Arch found?" Mary Ann asked as Jay shot her a look from the side.

"We never ever talk about that…unless we are ready to pull the sheriff in…and we may soon. But let's get through the first round of arbitration and give him a chance to confess. If he doesn't offer you a pile of money, well, may God help him…Then we call the law."

"Is that legal?" Mary Ann asked. "Waiting to tell the authorities?"

"Mary Ann," Rachel shot back, "you can call it 'legal' or 'illegal', but professionals call it 'leverage.'"

"Okay. Okay. Sorry to doubt you. So," she repeated for Jay's benefit. "We don't jump him with the tax evasion at the next meeting. That's for the meeting after. A new arbitrator has been hired, a tough little person." Jay and Mary Ann stared at each other.

Mary Ann put her hand over the speaker and looked at Jay.

"Wow," he said. "This is getting all Game of Thrones and shit."

Mary Ann looked confused and went back to the call. "I'm here," Mary Ann said.

She kissed Jay lightly on the edge of his lips and ran her hand down the side of his face. A white man on rollerblades smiled as he skated through their lust.

"When we get the new date, I will let me know immediately," Rachel said.

"Thank you. Do you know how much advance notice we'll get?"

"Oh, a week. Arch has mapped out the money trail. We know how it goes so that means we can get at it. He may not be at the next meeting—he's still on the Vinesteen divorce—but he'll be at the meeting after it. You know, the big show."

"The big show," Mary Ann repeated. "How long I've waited."

"Does it make those nights home alone worth it now?" Rachel asked.

"Oh fuck no," Mary Ann said. "That man owes me almost twenty years of living."

◘

He moving

...came the text from The Whale and Dashaun and

Ragz went running for HQ in the garage. The moment they had been on edge for was strangely still exciting though on video, it was just fat Jair at his computer.

Jair moving money was not exciting in itself. What was exciting was that a Wall Street firm in New York City could be penetrated and monitored in France while an operation on the ground could bring in two million for the team. This was global business, high tech and fast. They had arrived.

Jair's email was to a company in northern New Jersey, an import/export business that, upon later examination, never had any bill of lading filed in any port in North America.

Dear Giovanni,
Will be sending in a new order by
week's end. Many thanks.
Jerald Carlyle

"Wow," yelled Ragz. "Wonder what that means!"

"It mean you bent his coat hook when you dangling there and he ordering a new one…" Dashaun cackled.

Ragz was hurt and only after an OG tickle from Dashaun began to see the humor. The kid had no hint about how to be with an older man, no experience. He hung on Dashaun's every word and wanted to spend days with him, working out, working on the patio, taking care of the kids, hanging out in HQ. Nina just assumed Ragz would be around for lunch and dinner, so she made enough for him.

"He like a stray mutt," Dashaun said to her as they went to sleep one night.

"He's like a son," she said. "He like a mutt."

"Have you ever seen the way that boy looks at you?" Nina asked. "His eyes are huge and he never takes them off you, no matter what is happening. He mimics the way you act, the way you stand. Hell, he even wears Dickies and those holey old red Chuck Taylors. He loves you."

"Well, I don't want him to love me," Dashaun snarled.

"You don't get to say," Nina said. "Only God gets to say when it comes to love. It's God's decision. And Ragz loves you."

"Well, he ain't moving in here."

"He doesn't have to, D," she said. "He's here all day and he's been sleeping in the garage at night. Oh, you didn't know that, did you big man? He hides his stuff. I saw him using the garden hose to brush his teeth the other morning."

"What? That little shit…"

"No, you little shit." Nina was rarely angry. "There is a young man living in your garage fifteen feet from where you family sleep every night, and you don't know it. *No, you little shit* because you wanted to get close to Ragz and no closer. Well, *that little shit* need your ass. He need to know how to be a man. How to

love a family. It's starting and I love it. I'm up for this, D. But no one can save him but a man who has had the experiences you've had. He won't listen to anyone else. You grew up without a father. He grew up without a father. Your mother had a drug habit she paid for with sex. His mother have a drug problem she pays for with sex. You banged hard and almost died over and over and over. You don't want that for him. Saving him is saving your best young self."

Nina was finished. Her cheeks were flushed up high. She was staring at one of the fiercest OG's on the East Coast of the United States of America—the famed Machete—with tears streaming over the tears tattooed just beneath his chinky green eyes.

◼

The first meeting with the Arbitrator Dawn Long seemed to come quickly. The violent fluorescent light widened every pore as Mary Ann's legal team took their place across from the meat wall of Jair and his lawyers back in the Rosen, Guilden and Stern conference room.

Mary Ann had decided to sit directly across from Jair. This was a good tactic Jay had advised her over and over. Intimidate your opponent. Float like a butterfly, sting like a bee. What really helped her decide was Jay's huge penis. She had that well-fucked glow that no annoyance could penetrate.

Elder acne on her nose was gone. She'd changed hairdressers and with it color; now flipping a head full of expensive highlights like a Dallas blonde. She started going to Jay's mixed martial arts classes and was pleased that although she felt like a jackass kicking and spinning, her stomach was already tight and flat.

Yeah, she was ready to sit down across from Jair. What she wasn't ready for was the way he looked.

When a man and woman are married for almost twenty years, they see each other in many unpleasant states: puking, farting, going number two, getting number two on each other, prematurely ejaculating and having a baby come out of a vagina. They see each other the first thing the morning after and the last thing the night before. But Mary Ann was not prepared for this.

His hair seemed to be coming out in chunks. His head wasn't so much going bald as being deforested, as if someone were ripping out swathes at the roots with a backhoe. His eyes were red, tormented, and he had gained back whatever weight he'd lost when he first moved in with Carilee. This Jair Mary Ann knew and didn't. She felt sorry for him, the old mother feelings starting up again. What was it with Jair and his hair, she thought? It was biblical.

Noise stopped when the arbitrator, Dawn Long entered the room. She walked around the conference table, introducing herself in a pleasing baritone. She wore a pale pink pantsuit that seemed to rise at the waist where her back arched. Mary Ann marveled at the engineering. Her head floated just above the table edge, perfect black Chanel bob attracting attention so she looked even more big-headed. Yes, it was a balls-out hair-do and spoke volumes to Mary Ann. She would have called her the "Pocket Anna Wintour" but "Pocket Hercules" it would be.

"Good afternoon, ladies and gentlemen," Long said as Mary Ann noticed more meat sitting against the opposite wall. They had to bring a whole side? A rump roast wasn't enough? She smiled. Not cool; She was having an interior life in a conference room.

"...We are gathered here today....I just can't help that one....to reach an agreement to dissolve the union of Jerald and Mary Any Carlyle. For the record," she spoke into a recording device shaped like a Klingon warship in the center of the table, "in attendance are Attorney Rosen of Rosen, Guilden and Stern for the husband and for the wife, Attorney Rachel Rosen-thalerheim." Rachel and Ms. Long exchanged a warm nod that caused the line of meat to flutter and exchange curious looks.

"From reading offers from both sides I see that you are deeply divided on an equitable division of the marital assets."

"That's correct, Attorney Long," Attorney Rosen affirmed in his strange mezzo-soprano voice.

"Yes, Dawn," Rachel said. "And forgive me if I don't use the formal nomenclature as we are not in a courtroom. We're in a conference room. One as imaginative as the counteroffer of Mr. Carlyle's representatives."

The tiny arbitrator was unflappable. She simple swiveled her wee legs over the other way to watch the other side of the room of divorce lawyers explode.

"This is simply not true, *Dawn*," Rosen said. "Our counteroffer was fair. Mrs. Carlyle has not contributed any monies except a small inheritance that was used for education and is the only thing that can be counted as part of the overall equity of the marriage."

"*DAWN*," Rachel's voice came from deep within her body and seemed to carry a hot forceful wind, like a million women yelling at their kids: "I think we can list at least four major court decisions that despite the lack of monetary contribution a woman makes to a marriage, we can at least say that her time and energy is worth the $7.50 of the current minimum wage—that makes for $600 a week—a great deal more than the .04 cents a day of Mr. Carlyle's counteroffer."

"Well that right there is disgusting," the Chanel Bob said effortlessly and without rancor. "I see the financials and anyone can plainly see that Mr. Carlyle made over $300,000 a year plus bonuses. Why so cheap, boys?" There were no games for a woman who everyone tried to turn into a game.

"AND" boomed Rachel Rosenthalerheim before Attorney Rosen spoke, "Mr. Carlyle wants full custody of his son—his wife's very life's work—while literally leaving her enough money to live in a prefab condo that will blow off Long Island in the next global warming event."

With a tiny taste of her courtroom mojo, the pink side began to look at Rachel as if she was something besides a cast member of American Horror. The woman had real intellectual vigor, a fighter, an orator of the old school that brought the entire world's sorrows and triumphs to work for their trembling clients. Divorce and global warming. Now that was a powerful link in the thought process.

"Of course I want custody," yelled the patchy-headed Jair. "She's fucking a black kid. From Harlem no less! He's probably some kind of gangster. I won't have my son in that environment!"

"What!" Mary Ann erupted. "I can't believe you remember you have a son. And you bet I'm having the time of my life without you, Jair. You bet I went to bed with a young black man. He's got a huge dick. And it doesn't take a week to get hard again! Try 15 minutes!

"Good God. He's running all over our house jizzing on everything! That's sure to bring up the property value."

"You are so stupid, Jair. You learn that on HGTV?"

"Stop this!" Attorney Rosen said, his high voice again surprising the room.

"You left me! You left your son! Let's keep the role model department straight here, Fat Boy," Mary Ann shouted. "You left us for a chubster half your age. *Your assistant.* Isn't there some kind of sexual harassment law against that? A statutory rape kinda thing?"

"She would have to file the complaint," Rachel inserted, "that he forced her with the threat of losing her job. And be under 18, of course."

"Whole damn point is a ni...Nig....African American almost the same age of my son has occupied my position in my home, a home I vacated, yes, but do continue to pay the mortgage, utilities, and taxes on....I want that black boy gone..."

"*Black boy*," Mary Ann came out of her chair like a test rocket off the Nevada desert floor. "*Black boy. Ni....Ni....*" she sneered. "*African American.* Or is it the big dick part, Jair? So glad we finally got to down to it, finally got to the *nub*," she was staring at his hair now. "I thought I hated you because you were self-centered and greedy and fat. Turns out I hate you because you're ra....rac.....I can't even say it. You're the '*R' word.*"

The room gasped and the word "racist" was murmured up and down the line on each side of the great divide, the midtown Manhattan conference table.

"I am not!" Jair shouted. "Am not! Am not! Am not! Am not!"

THWACK!

A tiny heel of a tiny tan pump hit the huge conference table, silencing the melee.

When Attorney Long saw that she had control of the room again, she slid her foot wear back on. She'd been amazed at the men in her life who had become obsessed with her toes upon first glance. Tiny and perfectly articulated, men crossed continents to get her to slip off her shoes.

"THAT'S ENOUGH," Dawn Long shouted. "You, Mr. Carlyle, need to get in touch with your inner feelings about the other races of the world. For the record, this arbitration between Jerald and Mary Ann Carlyle will only continue after Mr. Carlyle has passed the State's Race Sensitivity Awareness Training Program. You, Mrs. Carlyle really need a lesson as well. I assign you to 30 hours of volunteer service at the nutrition center at the county hospital. You are about to see what fat really looks like and why it happens. You'll quit your rude 'fat boy' shouts. When you two have passed your respected requirements, please inform my office and we will set up you next mediation session."

She hopped down off the chair, legal pad clutched to her chest, bag almost dragging the floor, pushed her way through the glass and was gone.

◼

Two days later, Jay, Mary Ann, Dashaun, Nina and various kids sat on the patio. The adults were having sangria, a recipe Nina had gotten off Ina Garten's show that day.

"24,000 bucks and you see how fast Jair's hair fell out? I knew that Doctor Sharpe was a complete charlatan the second I laid eyes on him."

Jay, Dashaun and Ragz shot each an "uh-oh" look.

Jay said, "Well you told us to take the hair."

"What are you talking about?" Mary Ann said.

"I took something from my shower, something Nina uses," Dashaun said, "and put it in the shampoo bottle when we went into his condo to set up the cam."

"You took his *hair?*" Mary Ann said.

"You took my *Nair?*" Nina said

"You tole us you wanted his hair gone," Ragz added from somewhere behind their chairs.

"Wow." Mary Ann's eyes filled once again.

"Yo, Mary Ann, you still got feelings for him?" Jay asked without thinking he wasn't alone with her.

"Of course not," Mary Ann said. "No one has ever done anything so nice for me ever….making my ex bald again….it just the sweetest thing." She looked at Jay and then around at rest of them sitting on the packed little bit of brick: She felt nothing but love for all of them.

Mary Ann didn't understand it then but she had started to build her new family.

◘

Arch Noblach floated down the halls where the venerable Jerald Carlyle spent his days. Arch was after someone else in the firm, someone that helped old man Vinesteen squirrel away the operating budget of a small country offshore. Seemed this place was a furtive banker's paradise, Arch thought as he stopped at the coffee station.

As he hit "extra dark expresso" on the Flavia machine, a young man in a charcoal grey three-piece suit was alongside him, complaining about the coffee. Arch stared into his shoulder and mumbled back.

"Hi, I'm Jonathon," the young man said to Arch, extending his hand. Arch reached out and brushed his limp, fairly moist palm across it and returned it quickly to his pocket.

Bottum didn't think a thing of it: These money houses were full of people on the spectrum. They were great at numbers. Autistic. Asperger's. Bring 'em. Let them be brilliant down in the dungeons while we wow 'em up here, he thought, in these great suits. Can't let clients see short sleeve shirts and pocket protectors.

"May I ask you who you are here to see?" Bottum asked.

"Brian Leopold, he handles old man Vinesteen's account," Arch said into Bottum's chest area.

"Oh, he's right next to me. I'll walk you." As they passed Bottum's office, he said, "This is me. Take a peak in. I just had it redone."

As Arch glanced in, the tiny translucent filaments that some call hair stood up all over his body. There, in the middle of a rare Heriz Persian, was a huge 19th Century mahogany desk with leather inserts.

Where had he seen that desk before? Wasn't in New York. These corporate money buildings were institutional, not elegant, Arch thought, as he said, "a Heriz. Where did you get that?"

"All it takes is money, my friend" Bottum said, "and I believe an entire bonus." Bottum chuckled as only one Persian rug lover to another can: That was a $135,000 rectangle of woven wool.

"Interesting desk. I've seen one before, I think. In Paris, if memory serves," Arch said with the memory of those on the spectrum.

"It does," Mr. Bottum said. "It recently arrived. A gift from a friend."

"Nice friend," Arch said. "Now you just need one that likes to buy rugs."

In his flat emotional delivery, Arch might have as well as have accused Bottum of being a furniture whore.

"Well, let me help you on your way," Bottum said as he pointed him to Leopold's office next door.

◾

Moving again

The text came in early one morning around 7:30.

Dashaun made his way to the garage where he roused Lil' Ragz. They had built him a little bed with a half- fridge for his Cokes and a power strip for his multitude of gadgets. Man, could this kid ping.

"He moving," Dashaun said as he powered up. Ragz got out of bed and sat behind him in Avenger pajamas. The Hulk took the entire center of his chest.

"You kill me. You wear those little kiddie PJs and want to bang," Dashaun said.

"Nina bought 'em," Ragz answered.

"That figures. You her little boy now."

"I gots a mom."

"Where is she, man?"

"Don't know."

"Then for now, you got me and Nina. Never disrespect us in this house. We good on that?"

"We are."

"Now, what our baldy doing?"

"He's at his computer and it looks like his hair is coming back where Nina's leg lotion took it off," Ragz reported. Dashaun stared at the feed, eyes on Jair's head.

"Yeah, patchy but bad." Then he swiveled to his laptop to watch Jair type out his email.

Giovanni—
Adding money on order. Will arrive August 1. Sincerely,
Jerald Carlyle

Dashaun smiled the smile of a cat burglar who had just gotten news the owners would be out for 4 hours. He immediately picked up a burner and texted The Whale:

August 1
The Whale fired back with
Cheese moving?
Dashaun answered
Looks substantial

…and their phones went dark. Dashaun immediately called Jay and told him that Jair was making a financial move on the first. Jay then called Mary Ann who then called Rachel who then called Arch.

Unbeknownst to anyone but Mary Ann, a legal team and OG Bloods of the highest levels were working globally to get her money. She'd finally fucking tapped The Force.

She wished Jeremy a good day at school and sat back down in the breakfast nook to finish her coffee.

◘

With a point to fix on—August 1—Rachel Rosenthalerheim activated her Go Team, a tiny and tenacious a group as ever assembled anywhere to fight any foe.

First, she began petitioning Dawn Long for that date of the next arbitration meeting. Arch Noblach practically moved in: His computers and stacks of excel sheets covered Rachel's stacks of *New York Law Journals*, *Smithsonian*s and *Jewish Woman* magazines in the living area. Tubs of tempeh cream cheese and half eaten bagels tittered atop at least 5 editions of

Black's Dictionary, assorted volumes of the *Lawyers' Edition* and some folded sections of the *Wall Street Journal*.

Arch was working atop an empty pizza box on his lap. Rachel was at her computer in her office, the kitchen, which formed one side of the living room.

All the windows in the studio were open, car horns punctuating every question about Jerald Carlyle and his money and his mistress. *Fock you*, the love call of New York, would rise with bursts of Spanish, German and French shooting into the window and rolling around the airless apartment.

Rachel could smell Arch and Arch could smell Rachel: That's how hard they were working.

"The moment we are really going to nail him," Arch said through the beep-boop-beep-boop of an ambulance, "is as the money sits in the shell company. Banks have just gotten too good at helping people hide money. He gets it to a bank, it prolongs this by years. But if it's sitting in the shell, the Feds can spot it as soon as they walk in. There will be no business, no inventory, no shipping, no services. Just air."

"Banks have had a couple extra few centuries to get extra good at thievery and nonsense as expressed in the perfection of its most grotesque creation, The London Whale," Rachel said.

"Ah yes," said Arch. "The London Whale. He was merely a tipping point in the middle class's consciousness. Imagine *derivatives*, the most anti-American business practice known to man, and yes, he helped its rise. But who could imagine the United States government would allow its people to bet on whether a capitalistic endeavor succeeds or fails? Like a turtle race at a bar in Key West. That's our first black President, Bill Clinton. He made it so!"

Rachel had heard all this before. Arch liked Barack Obama because, as he said, when it came to black Presidents, he demanded authenticity.

"Oh Arch...." she had hoped to cut him off before his next statement.

"...and the Vatican! Now those are the serious moneymen in that organization, Rachel. They got more going on than Jack Zuta."

"Who the hell is..."

"Capone's accountant," Arch said before he turned back to his pile of excel sheets. "I've studied his work in depth."

Arch hadn't meant for that last detail to come out but there it was. Thank goodness at just that moment the ice cream truck parked beneath Rachel's window and their shouted conversation about the devil inside humankind was drowned out by the tinkly Jack-in-the-Box music from the truck.

As colleagues working closely in a divorce practice, good and evil was a conversation they'd had. And had. And had, as they watched perfectly good people fling themselves on the fire of hurt feelings and new pussy or harder cock, over and over and over. It was, they called it, the American way of death. But it paid the bills and kept the lights on.

Bing.

Rachel and Arch looked at their phones, which were dark, and then their computers in a synchronized head swivel.

"Hot damn!" Rachel yelled. "Dawn gave us the August 1 date."

Archibald said, a smile forming at the edge of his pale paper-thin lips, "that means the money will be arriving as the Feds inspect it and shut the shell down as a bogus company. Jerald's money will be just sitting there and ready to seize. We keep it in country; Mary Ann has a shot at getting it quickly and getting Jair to jail."

"My genius Archibald. You just get better and better at your work. You know you were brilliant on the Vinesteen case."

"Speaking of which, why do you live in such a tiny apartment when you get such huge fees?"

"It's *rent controlled*," Rachel all but shouted "You know how hard these are to get?"

Rachel looked down at her phone and punched it.

"Mary Ann. We have our date for the next arbitration: August 1. It's a perfect date because Arch believes there will be a money transfer that very day. That means we can call in the Sheriff."

"Call in the Sheriff?" Jay was licking Mary Ann's right breast, stopped and began to listen.

"Yes. Tax evasion is a crime, Mary Ann" Rachel said. "We will have to alert the authorities, the Sheriff's office, probably the FBI. They get grumpy if you don't tell them."

"The FBI?" Mary Ann squeaked. "That sounds really really serious. For tax evasion?"

"It's Federal," Rachel said. "He's moved money across international boundaries. They take this very seriously under Obama. Others? Meh."

"What will they do to Jair?"

Oh, they all get all soft before the ax falls, thought Rachel. "He may be arrested. They will question him, at least. His lawyers will be questioned. His colleagues. This will ruin his reputation, career and financial life, no doubt."

"As it should," Mary Ann said simply.

"You are gangster, Mary Ann," Rachel said.

"So I've been told. Thanks for the news. Will I need to prep to get ready? "

"No, you studied the fat fuck for all those years. That's enough cramming."

◘

Mary Ann related the conversation to Jay. He stood up, stepped into his pants and put on a clean t-shirt. She never ceased to marvel at how his cock seemed to brush the floor. Must be an optical illusion, she thought, the power of the mind to make a vision true.

He left the room and headed toward Mt. Vernon: This was an important day at headquarters. He knew Dashaun and Ragz were probably already bent over the screens, taking in details.

"'Sup, 'sup, what's our bald boy up to," Jay asked as he pulled the garage door up. Sunlight streamed over the two Bloods working the score, red rags on their heads bobbing back and forth in front of computers. Beautiful, Jay thought.

"Our bald bad boy has given the date of his next move: August 1," Dashaun reported.

"Good. What do The Whale say?"

"He says that's the day we drain the account. The Banker has his man on the inside, some guy named Bottum. Can you believe that shit, dude? *Bottum*.

"Anyway, as soon as the money hits the shell company, The Banker will take it all."

"What happens to Fatty?"

"He broke, I guess."

"Mary Ann told me that her attorney set up the next arbitration meeting for August 1. It all goes down at once, that day."

"He be broke and he won't get no girl," Ragz said, innocently expressing the reality of being male in America.

"That's a double negative," Jay said. "D, you ain't teaching him shit?"

"Not about grammar. So where is the drain gonna be?"

"I assume The Banker will oversee the transfer from Paris. But it won't be his hands touching anything. He is way too smart for that. No, this here is a Master at work and we need to watch, learn, think and do."

"Think and do? You been in your kids' coloring books again?" Dashaun asked Jay.

"Shut up, fool."

"If you two wants to be my Moms and Dads you have to stop fighting," Ragz said.

"What?" Jay asked. "*Moms?*" Jay turned to Dashaun. "You tell him I'd be his *Moms?*"

"No, no. That's Nina. He just got confused," Dashaun said as he shot the kid a threatening look. "Hey you, 'Squirt of Ragz,' shut up."

Ping! Ragz seemed to answer as he looked back down at his game.

"Yeah, so The Banker oversees the drain and he'll pass it through several legitimate Bloods businesses all over the world. Laundered money, our pockets, couple of weeks."

"Do you understand that between the two of us, we'll have over a half million after this hit?"

"Hello new Xbox," Ragz said.

"Lil' nigga, you gonna have to think bigger than that if you gonna have Jay for a Moms..."

"Shut up, Nigga. And you too, little nigga. Xbox, my black ass.....I want an Audi."

"An *Audi*?" Dashaun never ceased being surprised

at Jay. "An Audi? Now that some dumb shit white people car."

"Oh, you want me coming down the block in a Hummer like a bonehead drug dealer or some loser think he in Iraq or some shit 'cuz he got a piece and a Yankee cap. I need to replace the Caddy and want something reliable."

"Ain't no nigger I ever hear use the word 'reliable.' That's that white bitch talking."

"Actually, it Shenay that want the Audi...."

"Oh great. You got a black bitch wanting a white bitch's car and a white bitch acting like a black banger. You got some mixed up world going there, Jason."

"You looked around? Kinda mixed up anyway, don't you think?"

"I do, young Jay. I do."

"Mixed up," Ragz repeated.

"Shut up, kid."

"Shut up, kid," Ragz said, and they returned to staring at their monitors.

◼

August 1 dawned as one of those East Coast summer days where the air is as moist and unmoving as a fart caught in a jar. Hair laid flat. Wet rings moved lower down the torso and butt cracks grew dark and sweat- stained. The police dreaded days like this as more than one citizen would end up with a knife in the side for no better reason than prickly heat.

It was the perfect day to end a marriage.

Mary Ann rose early and chose her weddings, work parties and funerals dress, her own, she'd sometimes hoped. A pale shell-colored pink sheath, it brought the color up in her cheeks and hit her lower thigh in a way that made her legs look extra long. Her shoes had stiletto heels, razor points, and thick silver metallic bracelets around the ankles that created that sexy shackled look.

She bought all new make-up at MAC during one visit to see Rachel in Manhattan: pink eye shadow, black liner and candy colored lips that curved and plumped, the perfect vehicle to murmur "fuck you" at Jair. Her hair? A chignon for a day like this, of course. She'd learned it all from Jackie: Don't serve garlic before the theater and watch the weather before styling your hair.

She stepped up to the mirror and with a straight gaze, she liked what she saw. Sure, she had on a little too much make-up, but the MAC pink would play off the pink of her husband's legal team. Her eyes were bright, alive and interesting. She'd lost weight from sheer happiness. A sexually fulfilling life was one key to a small waistline.

Jenny Craig had probably never told anyone that. Get laid! Mary Ann thought. Feel sexy and loved! You'll drop enough blubber to make an entire person! Too many people made too much money on people being unhappy, fat, trapped and unfucked.

Mary Ann's cheekbones had sunk some and her eye sockets were defined, creating a more sophisticated, knowing version of her wife-self.

What a hoot. Had I only known what a bill of goods I ate as a kid, I wouldn't be standing here. It wasn't the candy; it was the magazines full of wedding dresses and beautifully appointed homes. That's what made me fat.

She pulled out a cotton swab, swiped it around her eyeliner, heard the xylophone and walked toward her cell.

■

As it happened, Mary Ann, Arch and Rachel arrived in the lobby of Rosen, Guilden and Stern at exactly the same moment.

"We are one!" shouted Rachel. She seemed to sparkle.

"Why so happy," Mary Ann asked as they stood in front of the elevators.

"Because today, the world becomes just a little more fair."

Mary Ann smiled as she climbed on the elevator and faced front. Arch and Rachel joined her.

"When do we call him on the financials?" she asked.

"As soon as he denies he has money," Rachel replied.

"Then what?

"I step out of the room and call the FBI," Arch said casually.

"Are they waiting outside?" Mary asked, voice rising.

"No, they're visiting friends on the 12th floor. They come here a lot, Mary Ann. Believe it or not, you are not the first woman to marry the wrong person."

She cocked her head like a Spaniel. "Think there is a right person?"

"Doubtful, but I mean that in a cosmic sense, for everyone," Arch replied.

"So why do Gay people want to get married so bad?" she asked him.

"I don't know," he said. "You'd have to ask one of them.

◻

Rachel, Arch, Mary Ann and Dawn were all seated when the pink wall filed in. Along with Jair and Rosen, several new faces had joined the crowd. The room quickly learned they were the firm's money specialists. Gawd, Mary Ann thought. Instead of drawing swords, we're throwing accountants at each other. How boring. She did notice, and approved, of Jair's modernist decision to shave his head. He looked *okay* now but who cared.

Soon he would no longer be her boulder to push uphill.

Rosen spoke first in his strange castrati: "Thank you for coming here today, August 1, for the record, to, hopefully, arbitrate and dissolve the union of Jerald and Mary Ann Carlyle."

"Oh, let's get on with it," Dawn's deep voice cut in. "Your attorneys tell me that you both completed your community service with plenty of time to spare. For that, I thank you. Could you each please address the room briefly about your experience? Mr. Carlyle, you first?"

"I learned that I need to unlearn some of the things I learned when I was young, that different doesn't mean 'bad,' that there is room in the world for everyone."

"Why, thank you Mr. Carlyle. Well said." She swiveled on her chair toward Mary Ann and stared.

"I learned how to use a popcorn machine to make popcorn for visitors and for the scooter people."

"The 'scooter people'?" Dawn Long asked and thought better of it almost instantly.

"Those gigantic, strangely-formed obese people in the hospital to have their stomachs stapled...'the scooter people'...they call themselves that as they wait for their lap-band surgery."

"Thank you, Mrs. Carlyle. Let's move on to the meat of today's meeting."

"It's rare," Mary Ann said under her breath as the entire left hand side of the room laughed and even Dawn Long, hardened arbitrator, smiled.

"Ah...ah....I think I need to turn this meeting over to my colleague Stuart White for a short overview of

Mr. Carlyle's assets."

"Indeed you do, Mr. Rosen," Dawn said.

Stuart White had a "hear ye, hear ye" quality to his voice when he said, "Beginning with the agreed upon asset of 1305 South Revolutionary Road, Westbrook, New York, Westchester County—herewith to be known as the 'family residence.' Both parties agree to splitting the proceeds from the sale of this domicile."

Rachel Rosenthalheimer was out of her chair—or as much as anyone built like her could be—when she shouted, "We do not!"

Across town, Dashaun intercepted an email between Jair and Carilee that said, "here comes the money slam."

That fat fuck was texting his mistress during his divorce hearing, Dashaun thought.

So he wrote,

Now

...and hit the button to text The Whale who forwarded it on to The Banker who went into a cozy corner of his club to over see this, his favorite part of the game, with a little peace and quiet.

"Mr. Carlyle's claim for one-half the house or any of the Carlyle family assets is ludicrous based on the misreporting of his income. One half the house, $175,000, and child support for two years from a man worth almost $2 million...?"

"Wait…what..." The line of suits exploded. This was not what their accounting said…. at least not any of the accounting they would be showing today….

THWACK!

Dawn Long's tiny black platform hit the top of the conference table. The room immediately went silent. Worlds away, in New Jersey to be exact, an empty warehouse was being raided by the local police and a man named Giovanni was being loaded into a police car for questioning.

"You, Mr. Carlyle, are worth $2 million dollars? How is this known?"

"By me, Dawn." Arch spoke loudly and clearly. "Carlyle was making huge bonuses but only bringing home a small amount because he was saving money to elope with his assistant, a young woman named Carilee."

Again the line of suits exploded as Arch put a copy of Jair's financial trail in front of Dawn Long and one in front of Attorney Rosen.

"You understand," Dawn said, "you should have filed these papers with both parties long before this."

"Yes, Dawn, but we were afraid Mr. Carlyle would head for the border…and not for fajitas, if you know what I mean…."

The little person stared quizzically at Rachel, decided finally she was making a weird sexual reference, and began to talk.

"This is a very serious offense you make, Mr.

Noblach..."

"Oh, we make it too," Rachel said, pointing to herself and Mary Ann.

"Your honor...I mean Your Arbitrator...I mean Attorney Long," Attorney Rosen said, trying to divert attention from the pile of spread sheets, emails and photocopies of pay stubs that had just appeared before them. "My client and his team cannot begin to address these accusations...."

"....you don't have to, to us...." Arch Noblach said as four of the young muscular men with crew cuts in Men's Warehouse suits entered the conference room, held up their badges, and with the voice of every television cop ever said, "Jerald Carlyle? Is Jerald Carlyle in this room?"

In a dark corner he paid extra for at L'Impact, The Banker began draining the account in the Caribbean Royale as four hot young FBI agents grabbed Jair and began walking him to the door.

"Help me!" Jair yelled at Rosen who yelled back: "We're divorce lawyers! We have some friends who specialize in criminal law....We'll make some calls for you..."

◼

Down the numbers went....oh, how The Banker liked this better than a nubby leather strap on a young man's butt.

1,590,690.34,

1,402,301.44,

1,480,854.88,

1,345,050.88,

1,300,303.54,

1,255,405.75,

1,100,361.22

1,000,000.00.

…and there it came to an abrupt stop. The next thing The Banker heard was

Ping!

And up came a smiley face from his sometimes nemesis, sometimes colleague, Arch Noblach, the human sheet of paper, the man who can trace the plan, Mr. Knows Where the Money Goes, that said,

"Sorry I had to take the rest.
It was too easy when I saw boy toy's desk."
—Arch Noblach

The Banker threw his head back and roared so loudly that several men in leather chaps turned to see why he was having so much fun.

In the conference room melee across the water, two small women grabbed each other and were under the table, happily discussing old college friends as they watched Jair being taken out.

And Mary Ann?

She had ceased to exist in the best possible way.

She no longer had Jair's 260 pounds of hate loose in the world and she was hoping she'd get some money, sooner rather than later. She had no idea what had happened in Paris but assumed it was in God's—or a really excellent OG's–hands now.

She walked out into the parking lot where the air had lightened up a little. She could actually breathe. She didn't know if she was still married or not and didn't care.

She didn't know if she was a suburban homeowner and didn't care. She only *knew* for sure that she was still in her prime, had a young lover and a healthy son. What more did she need or want?

As a beautiful smile split her face, an elderly black woman waiting for the bus smiled up at her and said, "why so happy?"

Mary Ann looked down, smiled even harder, and said, "I just became a free baby mama. What could be better than that?"

Her new comrade patted her arm and said, "I know that's right."

◼

The wires burned between Newark and Paris as The Whale learned that The Banker had been burned. A million dollars was the budget for The Banker's toilet paper so he made good on every dollar, laughing all the way.

"Bro, I wouldn't be so happy we got fucked over by a sheet of paper. Arch Noblach? I used to be a LION!" The Whale yelled.

The Banker laughed and signed off.

◼

Several days later, Mary Ann got the news that Jair would probably do some time at Club Fed. He didn't pay tax on any of the money and they could pin racketeering charges on him and his friends at the shell company. Jair, being Jair, got a reduced sentence for giving up two of his colleagues who were hiding money as well.

As everyone began to settle down again to regular life, a phone rang in a tiny shower with a huge orchid under a spotlight on a gleaming sink counter.

"Hello Arch," boomed The Banker. "Where are you?"

"Air Emirates to Dubai. I'm in the mood to play without taxes."

"Ah, Arch. But you are so good at taxes! I merely called to congratulate you on your exceptional game and your win. As they say, see you next time."

"Ah, the game. And yes, Banker, next time." Arch said.

And as he closed his phone and rubbed the mist off the mirror, a hand reached out of the shower mists to grab a towel.

There she was, Carilee, all moist and pink all over.

AFTERMATH

Dashaun lifted the garage door and light flooded over Ragz already working over a bank of computers and laptops. He had the phone to his ear as well, calmly demanding the latency be fixed on his hosting platform.

"In that nano second, brother, they gets bored and pops onto another motherfucker's site. I want speed. Speed is everything. Speed is living or dying. You know that, man," he said into his cell. "I'm also not that happy with the compression rate. It's taking too long to load our new shots." He spoke with an authority that seemed impossible coming from the same little ball of bawling bloody rags they had first encountered.

"'Sup," Dashaun said as he came up behind Ragz. "Man, we are out of beta and the analytics look great.

We've also got a killer one-click campaign that will really move product. Our subscriber list is increasing by 110% a day, great metrics. We'll net 5 before we've even gotten started."

"What's your mega data?" Dashaun asked. "You adjusting it like we talked about?"

"Yup. So far, Bloods Crips Banging Hip-Hop and Rap have given us the highest traffic. And, we see a surge when we run the blog."

Mary Ann named and Jay wrote the twice-weekly blog, *Black is the New Black*. Tales of derring-do on the streets were interwoven with beautiful, arresting homegrown black, white and Hispanic models in action poses all over Harlem wearing Banger Tees.

Mary Ann and Jay seemed to materialize from nowhere through the raking sunshine from the open door and were soon in the conversation.

"How many different products do you have on offer, Dashaun?" she asked.

"So far, six. *Thrillz Me* was our biggest seller that first month but BlackIsTheNewBlack.com is a CLOSE second. We's got walking ads for our site all over the country."

Mary Ann smiled. She was proud of her contribution and had just blurted 'black is the new black' out at one of their startup meetings on the pa-tee-o.

"My homie in Compton called and said he saw some white kid in Santa Monica wearing a shirt that said *Hire Jamal.* That one of ours."

"What's your demographic?" Mary Ann said.

"We shooting at the 18–34 crowd. By the looks of the names on our mailing list, white kids leading the way. T-shirts like crack to 'em. I mean, really, we have experience in this game. Suburban kids. Toe picker kids. Starbucks kids." His voice turning deep, like a game show announcer, "They can't get enough of Banger Tees."

"That the selection over there?" Mary Ann asked, looking at long shelves stacked with hundreds of neatly folded and labeled shirts. "Mind if I look?"

"Please," Dashaun said.

As she strolled along the shelves, she picked up shirts that said *Rollin' 80s, Piru Street USA, Don't Butter My Biscuit, Bangin' thru Life* and *You Best Not Be Married.*

Every one had BangerTees.com at the neck, more marketing mojo from Ragz.

Like long-fighting soldiers home from war, their violent past was bleeding out of Jay, Dashaun and Ragz. Words they never dared speak were spoken and a dread seemed to lift from daily life. They were and would always be Bloods, but their contribution was now legitimate. They had run the gauntlet and gotten out alive. They had a shot at old age though the odds were completely stacked against them as young black men in America.

All of Ragz obsessions with gadgets developed into a near genius level of understanding and use of the internet. He instinctively understood from day one how it all worked together and with Jay and Dashaun's creativity, they were now edging into the American dream. Their first dollars were sunk back into the startup, buying more laptops, a huge Mac for design, and the latest software that kept their internet store selling 24/7.

Mary Ann and Jay remained lovers and best friends.

They never put words on what they were nor were there any needed. Mary Ann had lived a highly defined life and look where it had taken her, that rock-bottom moment of twisted metal and flying donuts in the middle of nowhere without a friend in the world to save her.

That rock bottom moment on the highway with the church van had led to all of this.

Jeremy was now enrolled at Brown University, close to his father's minimum-security prison. Their relationship had deepened, become real, and Mary Ann was grateful that Jair was really a father now, really helping her son develop thought and character. Goodness knows, Jair had plenty of time to think now that he couldn't play with other people's money or with his hair. Prison food did what Carilee's prodding could not and Jair never looked better: he was back down to his college weight.

No one's children were likely to die now, collateral damage from Jay and Dashaun's actions on the streets. Bills were paid in full and on time. The sett had to respect the no gun rule in the garage and often came by to help and watch the work.

This start-up of Banging Tees showed them there were ways out, that what they knew and what they had gone through had value.

And every Friday, Dashaun initiated "Employee Appreciation Day." The sett would come sit around, talk shit and gulp 40s. They'd throw around new slogans for t-shirts in a "judgment free zone" so all ideas were heard. Their logo was a perfect rendering of the beautiful Peggy Sue, now on display in the garage as if it were the Smithsonian.

"Hey, Mary Ann," Dashaun yelled. "What size you wear?"

"A medium," she yelled back.

Dashaun got up and walked to the middle of the long wall of shelves and pulled out a small white shirt. It said, *Blood Brothers* and he gave it to her with great fanfare.

The rest of the room laughed and she heard Jay say, "ain't that some shit" from the other side of the garage.

She walked up behind Ragz and Dashaun as they sat in front of the computers and said, "I am so proud of you guys."

Ragz was the first to look up. He smiled wide and said, "Thanks. We is what they call the new economy. I read about it."

The rest of the men in room murmured "I know that's right" and continued drinking, talking, inputting, boxing shirts and talking to the UPS guy in brown shorts and matching knee socks who stopped in for the morning pickup.

■

ABOUT THE AUTHORS

Jason Davis is a Blood, O.G. of one of the Blood chapters, father of 4 and contributor to the celebrated, *The War of the Bloods in My Veins* by Dashaun Morris. He lives in Harlem, New York and recently received an award for his work in the community from Harlem Hospital for Youth Advocate of the Year.

Beth Wareham is an East Village housewife. Her favorite activities are laundry and folding. She is also the CEO of Shadow Teams, an entertainment company based in New York City and Los Angeles. She lives in New York City with her husband and cats.

www.ingramcontent.com/pod-product-compliance
Lightning Source LLC
Chambersburg PA
CBHW071128170626
46809CB00002B/535